LET'S PRETEND

TAKING RISKS
BOOK 1

E. SALVADOR

ISBN: 979-8-9903219-7-7

Visit my website at www.esalvadorauthor.com

Cover design: Lilith

Editing: Erica Russikoff

Proofreading: Britt Tayler

This book is intended for an 18+ audience.

For anyone who's here for the vibes and hot hockey players.

AUTHOR'S NOTE

Let's Pretend was intended to be a novella. I wanted to write something fun, cute, a little spicy, short, and a boy who's astronomically down bad. And I did just that "sort of." Everything as you read above is still very true except this isn't a novella, it's a duet. ***So if you're not a fan of cliffhangers, then I'd suggest waiting until the second book comes out.***

It wasn't my intention to split this story, I really wanted something light and short to end the year. But as I kept writing Sylas and Anna's story, I got sucked into their world, their friend group, the banter, and everything else. One thing led to another and a duet was born.

Now keep in mind, while the story is light and sweet there are a few things you should be aware of.

- It's intended for an 18+ audience
- There is explicit language and sex scenes
- Degradation kink(exploration): terms used "slut" and "whore" between two consensual partners
- Mentions of panic attacks and anxiety
- Alcohol consumption

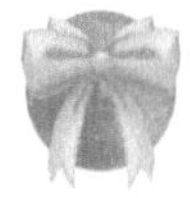

PLAYLIST

Empire State of Mind - JAY-Z, Alicia Keys
Time to Pretend - MGMT
Guess - Charlie xcx, Billie Eilish
Bed Chem - Sabrina Carpenter
Efecto - Bad Bunny
Me Porto Bonito - Bad Bunny, Chencho Corleone
Fetish - Selena Gomez, Gucci Mane
7 rings - Ariana Grande
Hands To Myself - Selena Gomez
Propuesta Indecente - Romeo Santos
Maldito Alcohol - Pitbull, AFROJACK
Are You Gonna Be My Girl - Jet

1

SYLAS

"See, this is where you made your mistake," Dad says, replaying Friday's game against Dartmouth. He pauses the video, zooms in on where I'm on the ice, and taps play. He talks over the video, nitpicking every minuscule move I make. "You had the puck in your possession, but then you..."

I tune him out, briefly glancing at my mom who sits across from me. I shoot her a *please get him to stop* look, but she is either oblivious or she's acting like she doesn't see me pleading because she says nothing. I assume the latter. She usually never intervenes unless she wants the attention on her.

"Are you listening to me?" His voice is sharp, and he snaps his fingers at me. "I don't know what you think you were doing, but the way you played Friday was atrocious. I need you to get your shit together, Sylas. I didn't spend—"

"Hi," says our waitress, Susie—no, she's not Susie. This is someone new holding a tray with our drinks on it. "Susie had to step away. I'm Anna, and I'll be your waitress for the rest of the evening."

My parents hardly acknowledge her, but Thea, my sister,

offers a small smile. Anna doesn't seem to take it to heart or care; she doesn't look offended, which is for the best because my parents are interesting, to say the least.

There's something familiar about her, but I don't know why. She's attractive and hard to look away from—that is, until her eyes meet mine and a small divot creases her brow. It's like she was frowning at me, but I'm not sure because she directs her attention to my parents.

I have no idea what that's about, nor do I care.

"Are you all ready to order?" she asks after she's placed our drinks on our table.

"No, we're still waiting on a few more people. They should be here any second now. So you stay right there."

"Yes, ma'am." Anna does nothing but smile.

I glance at Mom, but she doesn't meet my stare. When I look at Thea, she flattens her lips, probably to stop herself from smiling.

I should've known because there're three empty chairs next to us. *Fuck my life.*

"I thought it was just going to be us? Please don't tell me you invited Florence?" I grind my teeth at the irked expression on my mom's face, like I'm the one who inconvenienced her.

"It's not just Florence. I invited her parents, too, who happen to be our best friends. Don't make this about you." There's a bite in her voice, but to the outsider, it's meant to sound soft, sweet, friendly.

Just as she says that, Florence and her parents show up.

Our fathers have been best friends since they were kids; they played in the NHL together, and our moms met through them. And, well, Florence and I have known each other since we were born. Since then, our mothers have been scheming to get us together and marry.

Fuck that.

Florence Channing, puck bunny extraordinaire, is the biggest pain in my ass to ever exist. We fucked once and I'll forever regret it. Our moms keep feeding her this bullshit that we'll end up together despite me telling Florence time and time again I have no feelings for her. Still, for whatever reason, she won't move on. She keeps eating up all the shit they tell her.

The only reason they insist on pushing us together is because we're from the same social circle. So, it makes sense that we'd end up getting married, but fuck that.

As soon as they take their seats—and of course Florence sits next to me—they place their drink orders, and Anna speedily walks away. I've never been more envious.

Our parents talk amongst themselves, and thankfully, the conversation about my shitty game is long forgotten. Unfortunately, Florence scoots in closer, a sultry smile curling her mouth.

"Hi, Sy."

"Hey. I have to use the restroom. If you'll excuse me." I'm up and walking away before she can stop or follow me.

I slowly saunter down the hall that leads to the restroom, but stop in my tracks when I spot Anna.

"Hey, Anna," I call after her before she disappears into another room.

She peers over her shoulder, the divot returning with a deep scowl on her face, but when she sees it's me, it softens and she plasters on a fake smile. "Hey, I was just on my way over to—"

"No, I don't need anything." I stop and stand in front of her. "I just—"

She's really pretty. Black, pin-straight hair, bangs that slightly curve at the ends, round thin-rimmed glasses, pink plush lips. She has to crane her neck to look up at me, her head reaching to the top of my chest.

"You just what?" She looks at me almost with impatience and annoyance.

I blink, snapping out of it. I don't know what's with the indignation, but I don't ask, and I don't care. "Actually..." An idea lights up in my head. "I'll leave you a really nice tip if you accidentally spill water on the girl with the blonde hair. And I promise it'll be worth it."

She scoffs a laugh. "You are not worth getting fired over." Then she rolls her eyes and walks away.

When I head back, Anna reappears swiftly and hardly regards me. I'm not sure if I can call it an acknowledgement, but her eye contact lasts two seconds.

Funnily enough, it's my form of entertainment, because dinner lasts longer than I hoped. I fuck with her a little, like asking for more water, a different cup, accidentally dropping my fork.

It's shit, but she's subtly glowering and almost stabbed me with the steak knife. So I would say we're even.

But all my amusement ends when I hear about the Christmas Auction in a few weeks and Florence's desire to bid on me.

Fuck my life. I'm two brain cells away from stabbing myself with the steak knife.

2

ANNA

I TAP THE GREEN BUTTON TO ANSWER MY BEST FRIEND and roommate's call as I secure my scarf around my neck. As soon as I step outside I'm blasted by a dry, chilly breeze. New York never fails to remind me how bitterly cold this time of year is. Although I shouldn't complain. I was the one who wanted to move here—something that was made possible with my scholarship to King's Yard University in Manhattan.

"So, don't hate me," Jenny rushes out, a little winded.

"I swear, if you're bailing on me to have sex, I'm going to—"

"No, no. I wish that's why I was doing it." She heaves a fatigued breath, and I hear shuffling in the background. "My grandma isn't doing well. I'm sorry, Anna. I really didn't want to bail on you now, but you know her health has been—"

Now I feel like a bitch. "No, it's okay. You don't have to explain yourself to me. I'm sorry, I shouldn't have assumed. I'll cover for you. Have you already left?"

"You're the best. I seriously don't know what I'd do without you. And I am, just locking up now." She sounds relieved, but I still hear unease in her voice. "I'm sorry to do this, especially today of all days, but she—"

"Jenny, please stop apologizing. I promise it's okay. Do you need me to go with you? I can cancel today and reschedule for tomorrow."

Her grandma has been on dialysis for a year now, and despite her mostly positive response to the procedure, some days are worse than others. When those days happen, Jenny can't do much but FaceTime her because we're busy with school and work. So, it must be really bad if she's driving an hour to be with her.

"No, please don't do that." I hear a door shut in the background and picture her getting into her car. "You need to go today. You know how particular Michael is about us cancelling last-minute, especially for this family."

"Right, yeah, I know."

Michael's our boss and the owner of Elite Housekeeping. His company only works with the affluent families in New York, and with his astronomical rates, he's not overly understanding when it comes to his employees' excuses. Calling out last-minute could potentially lose Jenny and me our jobs. We get paid decently, and while we'd normally not even be qualified because of our age and lack of experience, Jenny's aunt worked for him for many years and put in a good word.

We proved ourselves though. We may not have had professional cleaning experience, but we've cleaned enough in our lifetime that he was begrudgingly impressed. Still, he doesn't fully trust us, so he tasks us with the apartments, studios, and condos of rich KYU students. It's insane because these are people I go to school with. I've seen about every designer item in those homes—names I haven't even heard of.

I've never felt poorer or more jealous in my life.

"I gotta go. And again, I'm so sorry, but you can keep my half. I'll just—"

"Shut up, it's fine. Don't worry about it. Drive carefully and text me when you get there."

"You're the best. Love you and will do. Bye."

"Love you." I hang up, slip my phone in my puffer jacket, and trudge away from campus toward the subway.

I don't mind cleaning alone, but the thought of said family makes my eye twitch and teeth clench. I never deal with them since they don't live there; it's their son who does, and he's never around when I'm there. I've met them, and they're exactly what I've envisioned a mega wealthy family to be like. Except for one member—she's not too bad. We haven't spoken, but she's not dismissive or rude.

But it's whatever. I don't dwell on them because, like I said, they won't be there, so getting annoyed over fictitious interactions is pointless. It's part of the job and something I need to get over.

Finishing with his bedroom is a mistake I've yet to learn how not to repeat. I dread it, and I'm too tired to find the motivation. Of course, I still get it done, but not without internally cursing at myself.

The penthouse is usually a mess, but nothing is worse than his bedroom and bathroom. There are clothes and socks—dirty, if I had to guess—scattered everywhere, shoes disposed in random areas, hair on the sink from shaving, empty energy cans and protein bottles littered on most available surfaces. It's hell.

He has more than enough space to organize his crap, but I guess he thinks the floor is perfect for it all. Don't get me started on his massive walk-in closet, the mess inside it, or the dirt his shoes pick up when he's out and how the area rug is dreadfully stained. Naturally, by the time I leave, the rug is spotless because that's what I get paid to do.

I blast the Christmas music from my headphones to drown out my agitated thoughts while I finish with his room. The last place I check before wrapping up is underneath his bed. I crouch down and am shocked to only find an empty water bottle.

I grab it and stand but jolt back in horror, almost tripping over my own feet. A sharp, small gasp scrapes past the back of my throat, but the rest of the air gets caught in my lungs, squeezing my chest. I fist my collared shirt, where my heart hammers frantically, and tug it away from me.

Removing an earbud, I stare wide-eyed at Sylas as he stands just a few feet away from me. "What the—"

"Shit, I'm sorry." He places a cautious hand out, as if he were trying to say he means no harm. "I swear I was trying to get your attention. I didn't mean to scare you."

"Then why were you hovering like a creep?" I step back, not because I'm scared of him but because I'm still trying to catch my breath. And something about being so close to him makes it hard to breathe. He's tall and broad—overwhelming.

He drops his hand, adding space between us. "You didn't hear me trying to catch your attention."

I'm finally able to pull myself together, but I can't stop myself from scowling. "So, it's my fault?"

"Yeah, you getting easily scared is your fault, but I'm sorry again for scaring you." It sounds like he's taunting me, with his wry smile and arched brow.

I'm ready to whip out an insult, but his parents pay my boss, who pays me. If Sylas reports me for talking to him a certain way, Michael will definitely not hesitate to fire me. Sylas's parents are two of his longest-standing and wealthiest clients.

"I'm sorry, I didn't anticipate you'd be here. I'm almost done."

Now I second-guess myself, worried I took longer than usual. On top of making sure everything looks brand-new, we have to get everything cleaned by a certain time.

"Don't be sorry. We got out of practice early and..." Sylas's voice wavers, eyes slowly perusing me. "Anna. You're the waitress from yesterday."

I can't stop the scoff from escaping my mouth fast enough and rush to soften my expression, hoping I come off friendly and professional. "Yeah, that's me."

His dark brown eyebrows furrow. "Did I do something to you? I'm sorry about yesterday. I was just messing around."

I don't mean to squeeze the bottle as hard as I do, causing it to crinkle and slice through the silence I let prolong. I could answer, but there are consequences, and like I told him yesterday: he's not worth losing my job over.

"No worries. I gotta get back to—"

"Quit the bullshit. I hate it." He cuts me off bluntly, the slight British accent more prominent at his impatience. "Just tell me what it is. It's obvious I did something to have you looking at me like you're close to castrating me."

"Will I get fired?" I stop twisting the bottle, pausing the Christmas music on my phone.

His lips curl up slightly at the corners, and amusement flares in his eyes. "I promise that won't happen."

I stare at him, deadpan, but that doesn't deter the playful expression on his face. It only annoys me, but frustratingly, it lessens the ball of resentment I've had toward him since freshman year.

"We had a communications class together, freshman year, fall semester. We were paired together, and you didn't show up for our final exam." My jaw flexes, and my fingers dig into the plastic, making it crunch loudly. "Not only did you not show up, but you didn't give me a reason or reply to me."

His brows scrunch in, his demeanor serious but thoughtful like he's trying to think back to that moment. I'm not surprised he doesn't remember it or me. But then his eyebrows rise and I see it dawn on him.

"Fuck." He drags his fingers through his thick, chestnut-brown locks. "I'm sorry, I had...that day...I dislocated my shoulder on the ice the night before and...how did you do?"

He looks genuinely contrite, and it's kind of irritating because of the memories of that day. I begged the last group to switch with me while I waited for Sylas to arrive and, thankfully, they agreed. I emailed him nonstop, asking if he was going to show up, but he never replied. He didn't even apologize.

"How do you think I did?" I snap. "I failed. It was our final exam and worth a big chunk of our overall grade. I don't give two shits that you don't remember me. I'm *pissed* because some of us don't have the luxury of paying our way through school. Yes, I know about you *passing* the exam you never took while *I* failed. So fuck you for that. It messed with my GPA." My face flames, and my fingers are back to choking the neck of the bottle. I can't believe I almost felt bad for him.

I walk around him but backtrack, tipping my head to look up at him because he's so damn tall. I'm mad and I'm going to get this off my chest while I have the chance. "And for the love of God, use your hamper, throw your trash or recyclables where they belong, and stop smoking, it isn't good for your health. You're a goddamn athlete. And fuck you again because, well, fuck you."

I stalk out of the room, vibrating with rage and nerves. *I just went off on a client.* He could've been lying about me not getting fired, but that felt good, really good.

I'm definitely getting fired.

3

SYLAS

I MASSAGE MY RIGHT SHOULDER THE WAY I'VE BEEN instructed to do by both the team's physical therapist and athletic trainer. One would have sufficed, but Dad not only insisted, he *demanded* they both be there to show me how to correctly massage and exercise, despite already having developed a personalized treatment plan for me.

My shoulder wouldn't be fucked in the first place if he had listened to them and let me rest. But he pushes and pushes because he can, because he knows better, because his son has to be the best and to be the best, resting doesn't exist.

He had me up at four this morning to train with him for almost two hours, and right after that, I had skill work followed by team weight lift. We have an away game so it was light, but my body is still reeling from training with Dad.

I prop my head on the bus window and continue to work my fingers along my shoulder as I scroll through my notifications. I roll my eyes at the messages that pop up from my parents.

Dad: You're not known as the best power forward in the country for nothing. Play exactly as I showed you and stop fucking around in defense. I will see you after the game.

Dad: Don't ruin my legacy, Sylas.

Mom: So excited for tonight! Florence is coming with us. She loves to watch you play. Why don't you get her one of those special jerseys? She would love that.

Ignoring them, I switch over to the security cameras. My parents pushed for them to be set up, since people would be coming and going to clean or whatever it is they do when I'm not around. It felt stupid at the time, but now I've never been more grateful.

I haven't cared to look because nothing has ever gone missing. But after my conversation—or whatever it is I should call it—with Anna, I've been wanting to see her again.

Shocked is an understatement of what I'd felt when I found she's been cleaning the penthouse and how she went off on me. I know I'm the dick of the century for what I did. I'm stupid for not remembering her and realizing why she looked so familiar at Clover's.

I never meant to blow her off three years ago, but when I dislocated my shoulder, Dad started his bullshit, and I was hit with a panic attack. It took me days to recover. It's still shit, and I get why she's mad. I tried to apologize, but she was done listening to me. She had her earbuds in, music probably at max because I could hear it playing. And she wasn't there long because she finished five minutes after she chewed me out.

On the screen, the elevator doors slide open and she walks in with cleaning supplies and another girl beside her. I don't recognize her, but what would I know? She probably goes to KYU too. I probably forgot her the same way I did Anna.

I pop in an earbud, but hesitate before I turn up the volume. Is this wrong? They're in my home, so it's not technically stalking or invasion of privacy. Right?

Turning it on, I watch them. Based on the topic of their conversation, they either know there are cameras and don't care, or they have no idea there're multiple small ones placed everywhere.

"...I don't know, I'm still waiting to get a call from Michael letting us know we're fired and blacklisted from New York."

Her friend laughs, and between the two, she's the bubblier one. "That's dramatic. I don't think Michael holds that much power. But enough about that, so..."

"No, Jenny," she reproaches with a groan. "Don't even think about it. I'll take the terrace and you—"

Jenny's smile widens, and she places a hand on her hip. "You're so lame. You don't even know what I was going to ask."

"I do, and I'm not going to answer." She grabs a plastic bag from the cart they brought filled with supplies.

"I just want to know. I promise I'll stop asking." Jenny interlocks her fingers, bringing them under her chin, and juts out her bottom lip.

Anna wets her pink lips, her chest rising like she's breathing in deeply. "Okay, ask me."

"Is he as attractive in person as they say he is?"

Is she talking about me? She has to be talking about me. I sit up and raise the volume.

Anna pauses, like she's considering how she wants to answer that, then rolls her eyes. "Yeah, he is, and it's annoying because he's also tall. Like, really fucking tall."

Jenny's face gleams with excitement. "And the accent?"

She clicks her tongue. "Deep and as nice as you'd imagine." She sounds pained to have said that.

Jesus Christ, talk about an ego boost.

Her friend hums in appreciation. "I'm jealous."

"Jealous?" Anna's face twists in a grimace. "There's nothing to be jealous about. He's gross, he smokes, and he's obnoxious. You don't need that."

My smile falls. I didn't used to smoke, but I needed something to take the edge off. Anyway, it could have been worse. I *could have* taken up smoking crack.

"Come on, we need to hurry up. My shift at Clover's starts at two." Anna grabs a few other things and heads toward the sliding glass door that leads to my terrace all while my eyes gravitate to her ass.

Fucking hell, she's got the roundest ass I've—

"What are you looking at?" Marcello "Marc" Galante, my best friend and right winger, plops down on the cushioned chair next to me.

"Nothing." I quickly shut off my phone, tucking it in my pocket. I take out my earbuds and place them back in the case.

He hums and gives a knowing nod. "Told you to stop watching porn on the bus. Wait until we get to the hotel."

"Fuck off."

He's always saying the stupidest shit.

"You look guilty." He shrugs, searching my face. "You still thinking about your cleaner?"

"Her name is Anna, and shut up. I'm done talking about that."

Marc had been downstairs in the living room when Anna went off. He has not shut up about it since it happened, and he told our closest friends because he's an asshole. And they're just like him, so they've brought it up. A lot.

But it's whatever. She's just a girl. She means nothing to me.

Friday, December 6

I intercept a pass, taking possession of the puck, and quickly skate past Michigan's defense. I stutter step the pass to Marc, giving me enough space to swerve before I wrap around the net and seamlessly shoot the puck.

The horn blares, the spotlights scatter around the arena, the marching band plays our anthem, and the sea of black, silver, and white goes manic, celebrating my second goal of the night.

"That's right!" I wave my arms, amping up the already loud, rambunctious home crowd sporting our university colors.

As my teammates swarm me, I skate backward, dropping my stick as my back hits the plexiglass and I bounce back. I smirk as they corral me, spreading my arms wide.

"The Punisher strikes again!" my teammates call out, hugging me and slapping my helmet and shoulder.

"That's right!" Marc bumps his chest with mine once the rest of the guys have peeled off me. "You did that, baby!" He hypes me up, slapping my shoulder and cheering.

We skate toward the bench, slapping our teammates' gloved hands before skating back to the center for face-off.

The last few minutes of the third period go by too quickly and disappointing for Michigan with a 4-0 shutout.

After interviews and our showers, we're still reeling from the post-game high. But it and the happiness I was basking in evaporates the moment Coach Viktor Ivanov utters the words "Christmas Auction."

Marc snickers, knowing how much I dread this stupid tradition KYU insists on continuing every year. I don't know exactly when it started, but it was decades ago.

Every December, the school's male athletes are picked to be part of the auction. People bid on them, and the money goes to charity. I know I sound like a dick for complaining about it considering the money is going toward a good cause, but it's the intention behind it that annoys me.

People bid thousands upon thousands of dollars just to show off that they can, using the guise that they're doing this to build connection with the players while helping the community.

It's laughable because most of the players here have connections and the means to bid—or at least outbid—on ourselves. But that's not allowed and we have to participate whether we like it or not.

I've managed to avoid the auction twice. Freshman year, I dislocated my shoulder. Sophomore year, I got a stomach bug. It wasn't an especially good time, but it got me out of being part of the auction.

Now in my junior year, I'm—I can't believe I'm saying this—unfortunately not hurt or sick, so I have no other choice but to participate. It's not been announced who will have to, but as captain, I know I'll be one of the four picked.

"I know you're all dying to find out who will be the four to join the other athletes on the stage," he voices flatly, probably feeling about it the way I do. "If I call your name, I don't want to hear it and no, I can't be bribed. Dress up, show up, and kiss ass if you have to." His eyes scan each guy in the locker room, then he glances down at his phone. "Everett Frost, Marcello Galante, Rowan Jovanović, and Sylas Lenoir Alves."

He has an excellent read on me because as he speaks my name, he looks up.

"It's one night, so make the best of it," Coach instructs us, but based on his stern expression, I know it's me he's singling out.

I swallow back the grumble that threatens to leave me as he switches the conversation to tonight's game. After giving us his usual celebratory speech, he bids us good night and leaves the locker room.

"Cheer up, princess." Berlin St. Clair, our defenseman, smirks. "You act like this is the worst thing in the world. It's a win-win if you ask me. You do your due diligence and you get laid."

My scowl only deepens as my teammates break out into laughter. "Fuck you." I turn, giving them my back.

Berlin might not consider it a nightmare, but I know who will be bidding on me.

"You know…" Frost, our center, tugs his jersey over his head. "You could always pay someone to bid on you. You have the money. I don't see why it would be an issue, and no one would have to know."

Why didn't I think of that? Sure, there's the risk of it backfiring. They could end up keeping the money or find a way to actually get me to go on a date with them, but…

"You're not actually thinking about it, are you?" Berlin cocks a brow, humor lacing his voice.

I shrug. "I don't know…it's not the worst idea."

Rowan, our goalie, regards me with a patronizing look but stays quiet.

Marc laughs. "You're fucking stupid. It's one night with Florence."

I flip him off, not saying a word to him but still consider Frost's idea.

"Stop mulling it over. It's not until next week." Marc drapes his arm around my shoulder as we step out of the locker room. "We got more important things to think about. Like skipping dinner with our parents to go to Salt. How mad will your dad be? Mine already threatened me."

"I guess I'll find out tomorrow."

He's going to be furious, but I'll think about the consequences later.

4

ANNA

Friday, December 6

"No coke or accepting drinks from guys."

Jenny places a hand on her chest, feigning offense. "What do I look like?"

"Like you're easily influenced and a 'yes' girl when you're drunk." I give her a pointed look as we take a step closer to New York's newest and hottest nightclub. We've been waiting in line for thirty minutes now, but it won't be long before we're in.

I had no desire to go out tonight, especially after the argument I got into with my parents and sister, but Jenny forced me to. She needs the distraction after being with her family, and she knows I need it too. Still, this is the last place I want to be. It'll be crowded and busy. I don't want to wait forever in line for a drink that'll cost an obscene amount. I can't afford to be spending money.

But it's one night and I'll be with Jenny, so I guess it couldn't hurt.

"Trust, after taking those edibles that one time, I'm afraid to even pop a Tylenol," she states with a shudder, making me laugh.

At the time, it wasn't funny, but now that it's been a year, we can look back on that night and have a good laugh. She was so overwhelmed by the edible she called 9-1-1, thinking she was dying.

I wasn't with her; otherwise, I would've been able to stop her from taking so many. She hadn't realized they take a while to kick in.

Major fuckup; lesson learned.

"I'm really sorry about your parents," Jenny says after a beat, her features softening.

I shrug despite feeling a shift in my stomach. "It was going to happen sooner or later."

Jenny and I met freshman year when we were assigned the same dorm. We became best friends though after we drank a few too many Four Lokos and trauma bonded. Three years later, we're still trauma bonding, but without the Four Lokos. They're actually part of our trauma now; we can't look at them, or smell them, without getting sick.

We're also on scholarships and part of the small percentage of students whose parents aren't swimming in money.

We quickly realized we didn't fit in when our classmates talked about visiting Monte Carlo in a private plane, the fashion shows they sat front row at, and the Birkin they were going to pick out.

With that said, Jenny and I know a lot about each other, like my parents' overbearing, controlling tendencies and her family's dependence on her.

"It's horrible they would disown you for what you decide to do with your life." She folds her light brown arms against her chest.

I lean against the cold wall and sigh, blowing at the bangs on my forehead. I knew they wouldn't react well to the news, but I didn't anticipate them turning their backs on me. Today was rough and it's only going to get rougher.

I stop adding and subtracting our bills when the bouncer lets us know we're allowed to go in.

"Just one night, let's pretend everything's okay." Jenny takes my hand in hers, staring at me with hopeful eyes. "Let's have a good time. Yeah?"

Once my mind is set on something, it's hard to shut it down, but I know if I don't stop thinking for one night, I'll spiral. So, I smile and nod. "Yeah, come on."

We walk hand in hand inside, the blaring music already drowning out my loud thoughts. The noise grows tenfold once the door shuts behind us.

Salt is supposed to give underwater vibes, and it's delivering—from the jellyfish-like disco balls that take up every inch of space on the ceiling and the intricately designed, color-changing seaweed on every surface, to the bubbles floating around us and the ripples of water projected on the walls.

"This is fucking insane!" Jenny shouts over the deafening music, gripping my hand tight as she marvels at the place.

I do the same. It's chaotically loud, trippy, and crowded. A college student's and stoner's dream come true.

We step aside before going to the bar, running through our do's and don'ts.

"I think we've gone over everything," I say.

"You think we look okay?" Jenny sweeps her gaze over herself and then at a group of hot girls that walk by us.

There's a bit of hesitance in her voice, and I get it. We're not wearing designer clothes unless you want to count the dupe Prada skirt I'm wearing. I bought it off a woman on the side of the street. It was originally sixty dollars, but I managed to get her to lower it to twenty-five.

"Yes, we look hot." I brush my straight black hair over my shoulders, adjust my snake-print mini skirt, and retie the string on my sleeveless burgundy crop top. It does nothing to hide my breasts, but I guess it's there for aesthetic purposes, and it also has a lace trim. "I know we're not wearing thousand-dollar outfits, but it's all about confidence...Or whatever those self-help books say."

She giggles and I feel her uncertainty fade away as she fixes her dress's thin shoulder straps.

"Remember: no getting drunk." I hook my arm in hers as we slip past the crowd and amble over to the bar, attempting to avoid getting bumped and stepped on, but it still happens.

She shoots me a mischievous smile, placing her right hand to her heart. "I promise to behave."

Though I need that reminder more than she does because I have a tendency to get carried away.

Once we get our drinks, we make our way to the dance floor.

I don't know how long we've been dancing for, but the only time we stepped away is to get drinks. The crowd seems to have gotten larger and tighter. Sweaty bodies grind against each other and get a little handsy. Fortunately, most of it has been girls, which I don't mind. There's something invigorating about girls having a good time together even if we don't know each other. It's the occasional guy who thinks it's cute to grab my ass that bothers me.

So, I do the equally cute thing and use the tip of my heel to stab their foot.

Jenny makes a gun motion to her head, rolling her eyes theatrically. "I swear they don't get the hint."

After I've had the pleasure of stomping on the fifth guy of the night, I say, "Thank God I chose to wear these."

The joys of being a girl. You want to look hot, but sometimes, you have to be in pain. I guess it's worth it if you get to share your pain with someone else.

"Do you want to go—" She stops mid-sentence, her hazy eyes going round at whoever is standing behind me. A lazy grin spreads across her face when her eyes bounce back to mine.

My brow furrows, but I don't get to turn before the guy behind me leans in and says, "You won't step on me, will you?"

I would recognize that accent anywhere. My brain has already thought of what to say, but my mouth works faster, thanks to the alcohol. "I don't know. Are you going to touch me without my permission?"

"No, of course not. I know better," he haughtily supplies. "I have manners and all."

I scoff a laugh at his pompous voice. "So use them."

I hear him chuckle. "You're going to dance with me."

"That sounded more like a demand than a question. No." I grab Jenny's hand, pulling her through the crowd until we find a good spot to dance in.

"That was Sylas. He just asked you to dance with him! Why the hell did you say no?" she asks, a sluggish laugh tumbling out of her mouth.

"Because he's a client and the last person I want to dance with." Freshman Anna would have caved at a guy's attention. Junior Anna knows better.

"He's behind you." She flashes him a lopsided smile before drawing her attention back to me. "I'm going to get a drink. Have fun."

"Jenny!" I gape at her as she walks away. "This wasn't the plan! We need to stick togeth..." My words get drowned out by the music and those singing. I raise my hands at her retreating figure. "What the—"

"I'm ready to try again."

I spin on my heel, staring unimpressed at Sylas. He stands in front me, wearing an amused smirk.

"No thanks," I clip, more irritated with myself than him.

It's hard not to gawk at him. He's insanely attractive, with a square stubbled jaw, dimples on each cheek, and messy dark hair that looks like he's run his fingers through. Then there's that stupid British accent. It's hot. Despite my brief analysis, I will not cave.

He drags his teeth along his bottom lip and chuckles, releasing it. "Just one dance."

Of course, he probably assumes he's going to get what he wants. They always do.

I smile at him, bright and big, and his own widens in response. "No. Fuck—"

As I'm about to turn him down, I spot Jenny dancing with a guy. She looks like she's having a good time and must sense me looking because our eyes collide and she smiles wickedly. If that isn't enough reassurance, she spins, snaking her arms around his shoulders, and makes out with him.

I should say no. Should walk away. I don't even know him, but it'll be one dance. "Ask me again and make it sound desperate."

He laughs, throwing his head back before he sobers. "Will you please do me the honor of dancing with me? I really, *really* want to dance with you and no one else. Pretty please, dance with me. Please Anna."

I pretend to be frustrated and sigh deeply. "I guess if you insist."

Sylas takes my hand in his and turns me around, pressing my back to his firm chest. "You're such a brat," he husks in my ear, splaying his hands on my hips. He squeezes them hard until my ass brushes against him.

"And you're desperate and easy," I counter nonchalantly.

"Fuck yeah, I am," he rasps.

And I'm fucked because that shouldn't have sounded as hot as it did.

One dance, then Jenny and I are leaving to grab takeout.

It'll only be one dance.

5

SYLAS

Friday, December 6

IT WAS ONLY SUPPOSED TO BE ONE DANCE. AT LEAST it's what I told myself, but then one became two, two became six, and then I lost track of time.

It all started when she stepped on Owen Kovinsky's foot. He rightfully deserved it for touching her without her permission, which I surmised when he came bitching to me.

I may be an egotistical, arrogant, cocky, womanizing show-off —and whatever else they say about me—but one thing I'm not is disrespectful.

But Owen is my teammate, so I did what any good friend would do. I talked to Chris, Salt's head of security who used to work with Mom, and asked him to kick Owen out.

He'll either hate me or be thankful that's all I did. Either way, I don't care.

His presence was long forgotten by the time I approached Anna. It took me a minute to go up to her, because what would I say? It's clear she dislikes me, possibly even hates me. So, I watched from a distance, saw four other guys attempt to do what Owen did, and had all four kicked out.

That's when I decided to make a move. I couldn't just stand here. Marc and some of the other guys were giving me shit about it; Frost even said he'd go if I didn't. He claimed he was only playing, trying to annoy me, but I heard the interest in his voice.

I didn't anticipate her dismissing me like I was a nobody. That might've been a bit of a bruise to my ego, but I've never been known to give up.

That's how I found myself in this predicament, semi hard and not wanting to let her go. I've tried talking to her, get a conversation flowing, but she's not interested in hearing what I have to say. She doesn't seem to mind my hands on her or grinding her ass on me, but I wish I could just talk to her for a moment.

"Congratulations." She pivots on her heel, smirking up at me once we've nestled in a corner to ourselves. I've got my back to everyone behind us, but I leave enough space so she knows she's free to walk away when she wants.

"For what?" I trace over her features, noting and memorizing how rich and black her hair is, how dark her whiskey eyes are. They almost look black, but I know they're not. Her glossy red lips are supple and, I'm sure, very fucking kissable.

"For keeping your hands to yourself." She slants her head to the side, folding her arms against her chest and causing her breasts to push up.

I'm going to hell because I stare long enough that I notice two things: She's not wearing a bra, and I'm certain her nipples are pierced.

I clear my throat, then move to lean against the wall. "What can I say? My parents taught me better."

"They must be proud." Sarcasm drips from her mouth, the smirk only indenting deeper on her face.

"Oh, super proud." I match her tone, but then I drop the snark. "Anna, I'm really sorry about—"

"No. I don't want to hear it." The playful expression on her face becomes blank. "I don't want to think about grades or work or whatever. I just want to have a good time tonight. So, let's not bring it up, and now that we're done, I'm going to go find my friend."

"Wait," I rush to say. "I—" I don't know why I'm doing this or why it even matters, but I know if I let her go now, I'll hate myself for it. I do a physical three sixty and extend my hand out. "Hi, I'm Sylas. What's your name?"

Her gaze flickers to my hand and back up to me, where she appears between amused and stupefied. I realize how stupid this is, and I know she's probably thinking the same thing. It's dark in here, but I'm close enough that I can gauge the reaction on her face.

She shocks me though when she slips her small hand in mine. "Hi, I'm Anna."

I smile and she smiles and something strange happens in my stomach, like a swarm of butterflies have been let loose. Or like a strike of electricity shot straight to my heart.

"Are you having a good time, Anna?" *Jesus. Awkward enough, Sy?*

But she smiles, all lighthearted and pretty. "Please don't be weird."

I let go of her hand. "I'm not being weird. I'm making conversation."

"Conversation?" She scoffs a laugh, and it comes out raspy. "Yeah, I guess I'm having a good time. My dancing partner is fairly decent."

"Fairly decent?" I'm taken aback. "I thought I was pretty good."

She winces, scrunching her nose. "I'm sorry, but you've been lied to. It's okay, we all can't be good at everything." She pats my shoulder patronizingly.

I chuckle, breathing her in and getting a hint of strawberry, vodka, and vanilla. "Not all, but most things."

"Right..." she drawls, slow and seductive. No, I'm hearing things. "At least you know how to keep your hands to yourself."

"I know how to do that very well. I may be many things, but I know how to be respectful and—" I get sidetracked when I notice a wayward strand stuck to her lip. I don't think before I'm gently pulling it away and placing it back neatly with the rest of her hair. "Sorry." I should move my hand away, but I don't. "Guess that contradicts everything I just said…"

"I don't know…" She rubs her lips together and tips her head down, eyes flashing to my hand on her hair.

"What don't you know?" I step a little closer.

"If it's considered contradictory when the other person might like what you're doing." Her words are dripping in heat, eyes hooded and dilated.

My heart rate might have just broken the scale to whatever is deemed normal for a pumping organ. It's racing—too fast, too intense. I'm having a hard time getting it to chill the fuck down.

"Do you?" I cock a brow, my voice gruff. "Like what I'm doing?"

She takes a step forward and drops her arms to her side. "Maybe."

I grab a lock of her hair, coiling it around my finger, then drag it down until it's next to her breast. Her chest rises a little faster than before and her nipple is now poking through her shirt, stiff and further outlining the barbell pierced through it.

I clench my teeth, inhaling a breath, feeling dizzy over her presence and the smell of her perfume. "Can I touch you right here?"

With her eyes locked on mine, she doesn't hesitate when she nods. "Touch me."

I close the space between us, walking her backward until her back is flush against the wall. "Where?"

"Anywhere," she replies breathlessly.

I release her hair and raise my finger to the outer part of her collarbone. Her light brown skin shimmers and heats as I glide it across the bone and inward before stopping in the middle.

I feel her heart pump beneath my finger as I drag it down until it's at the top slope of her breast. Her jaw tics, but she keeps her gaze glued to my fingers, watching and waiting to see what I'll do next.

I drag it over her shirt and around her nipple, teasing her until she quietly and impatiently groans. I smirk, enjoying her frustration, but I don't prolong it as I grab hold and pinch her nipple hard over her shirt. She inhales a sharp breath and fists the bottom of my shirt.

When I twist the barbell, she squeezes her eyes shut and tips her head down, and I almost miss it from how loud the music is, but I catch the muffled moan before it gets drowned out.

I lean in, my mouth above her ear, my thumb and forefinger pinching and twisting her nipple, occasionally pulling on the barbell. "How long do you think I can do this before you come?"

"I-I..." she stutters and drops her head to my chest. "Oh..." She moans again, a little louder than before. Like she couldn't give a fuck that there's a raging party behind us. Despite that, I make sure to shield her from everyone. I don't want anyone to see her the way I am. "That's never happened. Don't waste your time."

"Never?" I hum. My fingers are too big, but as best as I can, I grab the beads at the end of the bar and pull only those forward. "Well, I'm very good at proving people wrong, and I'm always up for a challenge."

She pushes her breast into my palm, releases my shirt, and slips her hand under it. She grabs my waist, nails digging into my skin, and I hiss.

"Don't disappoint me then." She lifts her head, and her needy, lust-filled eyes lock with mine.

I chuckle. "I bet I can get two."

She arches a perfect black brow, laughing. "Please don't make a fool out of yourself. Let's attempt one and then we'll—" Her lips part and a gasp escapes them as I thread my free hand through her hair. I fist enough of it to be able to tilt her head to the side.

I make it look casual. If anyone were to walk behind me, they wouldn't think anything of us. They'd probably assume I'm a guy hugging his girlfriend.

Little do they know...

"Stand on your tiptoes," I demand.

She does as I instruct, and I'd be lying if I said it didn't shock me. I half expected her to tell me to fuck off or something along those lines, but she does as I say without protest.

"Do you get off on that?" I whisper against the shell of her ear, blowing on the gold array of earrings that line her ear, my lips just barely grazing the skin before they descend to her jaw.

"On what?" She's feigning ignorance, so I decide to go along with it.

"Being told what to do and knowing someone could see what we're doing." I nip her jawline and tug on the piercing. She shudders against me, fingernails sinking deeper into my skin. "What else are you into?"

I make sure to nip every inch of her jaw. When I reach her chin, I bite down hard, earning a groan from her, but I know she enjoyed it because she moans a second later.

"We're hardly doing anything and I'm not wet."

"If I lift your skirt right now, you won't be dripping wet?"

As my lips drop to her throat, I feel it bob. "So you're playing with my nipple and I moaned; that doesn't mean I'm wet."

"You're not a very good liar."

"Never said I was," she quips, her breath choppy and fingers hooked to my waist so hard, I'm surprised she hasn't punctured the skin.

"So maybe you're not wet." *Oh, I know she is.* "Tell me, what gets you off?"

"Since you think you know everything..." Her words derail as a moan claws its way out when I release the piercing and flick the tip of my finger over the stiff peak. "Why don't you tell me what you think gets me off."

"I might make a shitty guess, and I really don't want to make assumptions." My hand holding her hair tightens as I feel her nail brush my raging hard-on through my jeans.

"Guess." I hear the smile and taunt in her voice.

She's testing and playing with me. I should stop because I'm afraid of what's going to happen in the next few minutes if she keeps stroking my erection.

I breathe, my dick throbbing, and roll my eyes back. I snuff out any space left between us from the waist down. She slips her hand away, letting me press my cock against her.

"You like being used and told what to do." I trail my finger across her tit, feeling the lace sewn on the deep V of her top. I curl it under the fabric and drag it back, baring her entire breast to me.

She gasps but doesn't slap my hand away. She only watches, her breath coming out in quick bursts.

"Beautiful." I stroke her deep rose–colored nipple, eyes fixed on the silver barbell pierced right through it and the goose bumps surrounding it. Her tit isn't huge, but it's not small either. She's perfect, like she was made for me and only me. "And slutty."

She presses her lips together and rolls them, then clenches her legs. Interesting.

"Do you like that too? Being praised and degraded? Did that make you feel good? Knowing you're doing something right but also want...no, *need* a little more? For someone to take control, treat you like a whore?"

She squeezes her thighs again and lets out a meek moan, her light brown cheeks burning a pretty shade of red.

"You're quiet, and I assume that's not normal for you. So, you like it, but you're not sure if you should?" I tip my head to the side, studying the tiny bead of sweat between her brows. I lean forward again, rubbing myself against her. "Don't be embarrassed. No one else will know. If it makes you feel any better, I've always been good about keeping secrets."

Words don't leave her mouth, but heady moans do before they turn into desperate whimpers. She's chasing it; she's almost there. Fuck.

"You've got a great body. Just look at how I'm using it." I continue to grind myself against her, my erection tenting my jeans. It's uncomfortable, but the pleasure makes up for it. "Fucking...beautiful..." I drawl roughly, slowing down only because I feel like I'll come and that's not about to happen.

"Right, pretty girl?" I pinch her nipple harshly and she yelps. "You've got a fetish for being used." I add more pressure, my voice low, authoritative. She can't help but peer up at me through her thick lashes as she nods sheepishly then stiffens.

I force myself to stop rubbing her as she jerks forward. Her entire body shudders and she releases moan after moan. I hold her with one arm while my other hand stays on her nipple.

After a moment, she's panting, chest rising haphazardly and hair sticking to her temple.

"One," I say as I bring my hand between her thighs. "Spread them."

We're in a secluded corner of the club, not entirely away from everyone because I can feel people passing by but we're far away enough they wouldn't know what we're doing. Or at least suspect it. Maybe we're getting cocky, maybe we shouldn't do this but she easily listens and does as I instruct. My mouth waters and my dick only throbs harder as I drag my finger over the wet lace covering her drenched, slick pussy.

I'm tempted to finger her, but I don't. Once my fingers are wet enough, which doesn't take long, I raise them to her nipple and smear her arousal all over them.

"It's easier to play with you like this."

Her eyes are shot with lust and adrenaline. She doesn't say a word, eyes fixed on my fingers as I play with her, use her, and degrade her.

"Funny how you said you weren't *wet*," I mock, clicking my tongue. "But since you're not, I'm going to need you to spit."

Her face flames with shame, but I only grin. Her cheeks hollow a little, like she's gathering her saliva, then she purses her lips just a tad and her saliva trickles out like a waterfall onto her chest. I use it to lather her entire breast, making sure I put extra attention around the piercing.

"Who needs a pet when I could have you?" I might've over-stepped, but my cock and her clenched thighs don't agree. "I should get you a collar, maybe a leash, walk you like a dog, fuck you like one too."

Her nails dig into me. This time, I'm sure she's pierced through the skin. But I don't dwell on it because I'm experiencing something I never have.

I'm coming and I can't get myself to stop.

An electric surge shoots down my spine and I tense, my cock pulsing uncontrollably as I continue to come in my briefs. My eyes flutter and roll back and my hold on her nipple tightens. I hear her whimper, moaning soft yeses, before we both go slack.

A minute then another and I'm pulling back slightly to find her staring wide-eyed up at me. The question *What did we just do?* is written all over her face, and I know it's on mine too.

I've never done this...it just...came naturally to me...and she was here...and I was...holy fuck.

Did that really happen?

I look down and sure enough there's a wet stain on my jeans.

Fuck.

"Two..." My mouth goes dry.

She lifts the satin fabric over her breast and sidesteps me. "I-I should go."

At lighting speed, she's off before I can get in a word. What just happened?

6

ANNA

"Don't you dare fail me now." I smack my barely-hanging-by-a-thread handheld mixer. The only beater I have gets stuck in the mountain of dry ingredients before it stops working altogether. "*Pinche, pu—*" It releases a soft whir before stuttering awake and spinning like its life depends on it.

I blow out a heavy breath, fanning my bangs away from my face. They land back on my forehead, making it itch. I blow at them again in hopes they'll move direction, but like the last seven times, they land in the same spot.

Note to self: hide scissors before drinking.

Brushing them away with my wrist, I draw my gaze to the TV where *The Great British Baking Show: Holidays* is playing, then let my eyes roam over my small apartment.

It might as well be called a cardboard box because of the limited space. It's embarrassing how much we're paying for 750 square feet. Not to mention the view is...substandard at best.

But on the positive, the rats are friendly and the neighbors are nice-ish. All things considered, this is New York, so I can't complain. I've always wanted to live in the big city. I came from Nowhere, North Carolina, so I'm living the dream, if you ask me.

"*Te juro*—" Jenny bursts through the door, grumbling and mumbling a string of curse words in Spanish. "If they don't fix that goddamn elevator, I swear I'm not paying rent. Fuck Jerry." Our landlord. "Fuck the elevator." It's been breaking down every three months. "Fuck Christmas." She doesn't mean that. "Fuck the rich." She definitely means that. "Fuck everyone." Not everyone. "Fuck the elevator again. And fuck me for agreeing to live on the eighth floor." We were two desperate and broke college students trying to find a decent apartment close to the university and our jobs. We took the first thing that worked for us without realizing it wasn't as great as we'd initially thought.

Her frustration shouldn't amuse and somewhat alleviate my stress, but it does.

She slams the door shut, kicks her shoes off, and sucks in a breath. Her furious light-brown eyes meet mine then skid to the baked goods scattered across the kitchen and living room.

I touch my nose in an instant, shouting, "You first!"

A millisecond later, she's mirroring what I'm doing and saying, "Dammit, Anna, no. I had a shit shift, I don't want to—"

I give her a pointed stare. "You know the rules. You're the one who set them."

We've only known each other for three years, but in that short time, we've become very good at reading the room. A tiny facial expression or a single word is all it takes for us to know something is wrong. Though right now it's a given with all the pastries I've got laid out. There's so many, I could feed all the tenants in our complex, and she's cursing in Spanish, so I know it's serious.

"Wait, before you start." I turn the mixer off and place it down as she removes her puffer and all the layers she's got on to keep her warm. I grab a glass and pour her favorite drink. "I made you *coquito*."

Her bottom lip juts out and her entire body softens, the tension dissipating like it was never there. "You are one of a kind. I love you and I didn't mean any of those things I said about you in my head just a second ago."

I grin as she takes it from my hand and inhales it. She sighs, and when she takes a sip, her brows hike up and she takes another.

"I figured you would need the extra alcohol." I didn't hold back when I added both rums. Not only because I knew my Puerto Rican best friend would need it, but because I also need it. "Oh, and I made flan."

"It's unfortunate how much I like men because I would make you mine in a heartbeat."

"I know…" I grab my own cup and chug the remaining half of the white liquid.

"Jesus, is it that bad?" She eyes me incredulously as I pour myself more *coquito*.

I'd never tried or made this until I met Jenny. Usually during the holidays in my Mexican household, we'd make *champurrado*, *ponche*, *atole*, or *abuelita chocolate*. So attempting *coquito* was like opening a treasure chest full of gold.

"Wait, does this have something to do with Sylas?"

I turn to hide my face as it burns. I'm sure my cheeks are pink, and that never happens. I'm usually good about hiding my emotions, but ever since Salt two days ago, my face feels like it's been set next to a furnace.

"Well…" I take a sip, but the cold drink does nothing to cool my insides.

"Wait!" I hear her run, footsteps heavy as she shuffles her things around. "Don't tell me anything. I'm going to shower! You're going to finish doing what you're doing and then we're going to drink and put up the rest of the decorations!" She slams our shared bathroom door shut before I get to respond.

She's done with her shower in record speed. Though she did wash her hair yesterday, so she got to skip that step.

Jenny tells me everything she endured today. I've experienced my share of shitty customers, from working at the restaurant, housekeeping, to tutoring rich college students who couldn't give a single fuck about school and the customers I sell my baked goods to.

Despite that, I'll take it over having to work in retail during the holidays. Unless things worsen, then I'll find myself at the register next to her.

We finish setting up the cheap little decorations we bought at the dollar and thrift stores and finally start on the tree.

The fireplace on the TV crackles and "Christmas Eve/Sarajevo" by the Trans-Siberian Orchestra plays. It feels sort of fitting to how everything played out that night.

Three sips for liquid courage, I recount in full detail what happened because TMI doesn't exist in our friendship. With every bit of information I give Jenny, her lips and eyes widen, and her hands stop working.

A few minutes later, I'm finished with my *coquito* and feel buzzed and turned on.

"Say something." I grab my cup and pour the ice into my mouth. I anxiously chew on it, waiting for her to give me a sign of life. She's so still, she could pass as a statue. "Jenny!"

She presses her lips together and brings her hand to her mouth, covering it as her squeals of *yes, yes!* slip out.

"What?" I pour the rest of the ice into my mouth, chewing faster. "What?"

"Anna Maria Lopez!" She exhales a breath and squeals again. "I'm sorry, I'm—wait." She drops her hand, her face the most serious I've ever seen it. "But you wanted this, right? Because if you didn't, I don't care who he is, I'll kill him."

I drag my pullover off and put my hair in a ponytail, stalling. "What would you think of me if I told you I liked it *a lot*." I whisper that last part.

I'm never nervous about opening up to Jenny. I know whatever I share with her, she won't make fun of me. So, it's not that I'm wary of her judging me, but rather it's me accepting what I've been denying since that night with Sylas.

"Bitch." She stares, perplexed and taken aback. "Do you know who I am? I don't view you any different because you enjoyed it. Is this why you've been acting weird?"

I go and grab the rest of the coquito and flan, knowing I'm going to need it. The ornaments are long forgotten as I hand her a spoon and we sit on the floor and pour more of the white liquid into our cups.

"Yeah..."

"You have nothing to be embarrassed about," she says before she stuffs a mouthful of the flan in her mouth. *Funny, he said that too*. "Kinks are normal. Sure, they're not deemed that by society because you know they have a 'standard' for what is." She rolls her eyes. "But it's not like you're hurting anyone or committing crimes. You're just getting off by getting used and being called a whore."

This is why I love her. There's no judgment; just a girl making her best friend feel at ease.

"I know..." I try to formulate the right sentence to express how it made me feel, but there are so many words wanting to come out all at once. I grab a spoonful of flan and then another before the words finally settle into a sentence. "When he pinned me to the wall, it didn't feel like he was caging me. It felt like he was making sure no one else could see me. And he was careful when he pulled my shirt back." My pulse thickens and drops between my thighs. Another sip and I carry on. "And his words..." I huff out a wanton breath. "They were demeaning, but I liked them so much, I wanted to hear him say more. Call me more names."

I squeeze my thighs once, remembering what he said word for word. "'Who needs a pet when I could have you. I should get you a collar, maybe a leash, walk you like a dog, fuck you like one too.'" I take another sip, but this feels heavier than the last because warmth courses through my veins and I don't feel as tense as I did a second ago.

An image sparks in my head, a picture I was doing my best not to visualize, but the alcohol is good about drowning my ability to care. I can see it clear as day.

A collar. Sylas fucking me doggy-style.

"Goddamn, Anna."

I drop my hands to my lap. "Did you picture it too? Is it wrong that I want that? Jesus, that can't be okay, can it?"

"It's very much okay, as long as you're enjoying and consenting. Don't be embarrassed," she scolds. "Tell me more."

A sluggish smile curls my lips. "'You've got a great body. Just look at how I'm using it' is what he said while he was rubbing his dick against me." I bury my flushed face in my hands and grin before continuing. "You know how disgusting it would be if anyone else would have done that? But he does it, and I'm fucking melting and begging for more."

"*Dios*," Jenny mumbles, fanning her face as she drinks half of her cup. "And all of this happened inside Salt?"

I nod. "It was dark and no one was around. He moved my hair, and you know how the saying goes: one thing led to another."

"Does this mean you and Sylas are going to..." Her black eyebrows perk up, a sly, lopsided grin stretching across her face.

"No, it was a one-time thing. It also doesn't change who he is. I'm sure he's already forgotten about me by now." Like he did three years ago. "It's better that way. For all I know, I could've been some sort of bet or God knows what."

Now she sobers up. "You don't think he—"

Something heavy settles in the middle of my throat and suddenly my body feels tight and my head spins. "No, but you know how weird rich people are. When they're bored, they play games, and athletes *love* their games."

Jenny snorts. "Okay, you've been watching too much TV. I really don't think it's like that. I'm sure if that had been the case, we'd know about it now."

"I know."

I don't want to use the *poor girl, rich guy* cliché bullshit and pretend a girl like me couldn't be noticed by a guy like him. Because I've been noticed and I've fucked around with said rich guys, but one cliché that remains is that they're all the same. Same entitled dicks who think they're untouchable. And unfortunately, they have the kind of money that makes them untouchable.

Which is why it was a one-time thing that can never happen again. Whatever I felt must've been a blip, a necessary deviation to distract me from how stressed and broke I am, and from how close I was to calling my parents. I would've hated myself if I'd called them.

Jenny must know I'm done talking about it because she veers the conversation to my journal on the coffee table. She picks it up and opens it right where I left the pen.

"Can't wait for the day all these recipes are in a cookbook." She drags her finger along the page, probably tracing over my drawings.

If I love something I've cooked or baked, I draw it in my sketchbook. I don't know if I'll ever have my own book with recipes, but that doesn't stop Jenny from hyping me up and making me believe I will.

"And when they are, you'll get the first copy." I grin, imagining it actually happening.

7

SYLAS

Monday, December 9

I CHECK UNDER MY BED, MAKING SURE THERE ARE NO stray socks or that a bottle didn't roll down there. Minus the minimal dust, it's clear.

I'm not doing this for any other reason but to be tidy. I realized a few days ago I should make an effort to stop being disgusting. It wasn't my intention, but between practicing with Dad, then my team, games, and classes, cleanliness has been the last thing on my mind.

So I'm trying to amend that, or at least do better. Now that fall semester has ended and it's officially winter break, I won't have to worry about homework or hockey after tonight. We'll have practices here and there, but it won't be anything heavy or mandatory until the end of the month. There's practice with Dad, but that's about it.

Speaking of games, I need to meet up with the team soon to review film against the school we're facing off against.

I do a final check—again, just to be sure. Not because Anna's about to show up to clean or anything. She's supposed to be here around noon, I think. I'm just trying to end the year off right or whatever.

As I step into the living room, I hear the elevator door ping and slide open. Two feminine voices float around, one energetic and the other soft and raspy.

I squeeze my eyes shut, forcing the memory of her throaty moans away from my mind.

"I think I'm going to have to get another job. What I make isn't enough to cover everything," I hear Anna say. "I think—"

She stops in her tracks, head jerking back as her gaze meets mine. Brows scrunching in and lips pinched tight, she stares at me.

"Oh, hey?" Shock rises in Jenny's voice. "Uh...Anna." She turns to look at her friend who's still staring at me with a slight scowl on her face. "Did we get the dates wrong?"

"No," I reply before she does. "I'm leaving now. I came to pick something up."

It's a lie, but it's the only one I could come up with.

"Do you want us to step out?" Anna blinks and regards me again, a different expression on her face this time. I'm not sure what it is, but it's less intimidating.

I shouldn't have assumed, but I thought maybe seeing me would have flustered her a little, or that her cheeks would have turned that pretty shade of pink I saw Friday. But she's not flustered nor is she blushing. Instead, she's...impassive.

"No." I'm so thrown off my game. This never happens. Why do I feel confused? I degraded her, but it feels like it was the other way around. "Can I talk to you?"

Her mouth parts and a divot appears between her black brows. "No, we need to get done by—"

"I've cleaned up a bit. It's nowhere near as good as you do." That sounds so wrong. Saying that makes me seem like an asshole. "But it's, uh, clean."

She and her friend wear the same astonished look. Still, I think she's going to say no when the surprise wears off a second later. "We still have to—"

"It's fine, Anna. I got it." Jenny cuts her off, waving a hand at her to go away, and she flashes me a small smile that feels a little mischievous.

"I promise I won't take long," I add, hoping it'll be enough to convince her.

She looks like she's on the fence, but then she reluctantly agrees. "Three minutes."

"I'll make it two." I smirk at her, and she glares at me like I'm a nuisance. Which is funny considering how she let me touch her Friday night, but I digress. "Mind if we talk on the terrace?"

She gives me a half shrug and zips her jacket back up. I gesture for her to go first and train my eyes on the back of her head, not letting it stray down to her ass.

Once I shut the sliding glass door behind me, breathing becomes strangely difficult. She's beautiful in the way that makes standing in front of her hard to believe.

Her thick black hair is pulled back in a sleek ponytail, and her bangs settle on her forehead. Her olive-toned skin looks just as soft as it felt that night. And as for the rest of her, it's probably for the best that I don't stare too hard.

The scrunch in her nose draws me out of my reverie. "Have you been smoking?" She appears so disgusted that I feel self-conscious for a moment.

"Calms my nerves." It's either that or hyperventilating from a panic attack, but I don't tell her that.

"What are you nervous about?" Her face goes neutral, but I spot the tinge of curiosity.

"I have a game tonight." *My father will be criticizing every microscopic thing I do. If we don't win, he'll have me on the ice until I throw up.* Yeah, that's too much to share with someone who I don't know. Someone who won't give a fuck. Not that I've ever shared it before, not even my sister, Thea. But despite how much I hate his methods, I wouldn't be at this level if it weren't for them.

"You know, it's not good for your health."

"You're concerned about my health?" I tuck my cold hands in my pockets.

She blankly stares at me. "No. I don't care. I'm stating the obvious. Seems like that's something you should be worried about."

"But then I wouldn't have something to calm my nerves." I lean against the glass, crossing one ankle over the other.

"There are many other ways to deal with nerves that don't involve a cigarette."

"Like?" I arch a brow. "What would you suggest? How do you calm yours?"

Does she even have any? She seems like a sure person, someone who doesn't crumble under pressure.

She rolls her lips together, glancing away, and I assume it's because she's thinking about it, but I realize it's to stop herself from smiling.

She sighs but I hear the tiny chuckle that escapes her mouth. "I...bake. Yeah, that's what I do. I bake."

It sounds like she just thought of that on the spot. "Bake like baking food or getting baked?"

Anna scoffs but smiles a little, making me feel proud that *I* did that. "I don't smoke weed. At least not anymore, but that's beside the point and not what I meant. I meant food."

"Did you really, or is there something else? Because I feel like there's something else you don't want to share with me and that's rude."

"Rude? How's that rude?"

"You stand there judging me for smoking a cigarette that isn't harming anyone—"

"But yourself." She gives me a pointed stare.

"That isn't harming anyone," I repeat, ignoring her. "Then you said there are many ways to deal with calming my nerves, but you haven't given me something solid, and your answer sounds like a load of bullshit. I'm sure you bake, but I don't think it's something you actually do to calm your nerves. Or am I wrong?"

She rolls her eyes, not like she's annoyed but like she's been caught in her lie. "I do bake to calm my nerves but I also—We're past the two-minute mark." She changes the subject. "And it's freezing out here, so if you don't mind, I need to go back inside to—"

"I picked up after myself. I swear it's not as bad as it used to be." I pause and inhale, struggling to breathe again and not grab another cigarette. "I'm sorry about how I left things, but I promise from now on, I'll be better about cleaning up."

Her brows shoot up and she stands straighter. "Don't worry about it. This is what I get paid to do." She goes quiet like she's contemplating something. "Thanks for not getting me fired."

The tension in my body evaporates. "I told you that wouldn't happen, but that's actually why I wanted to talk to you. I'm sorry about three years ago. I had nothing to do with the grades or—"

"Let's forget it happened and never bring it up. It doesn't matter anymore. I shouldn't have mentioned it. I'm sorry about all the fuck-yous—well, no, some of those were deserved." The amused tone in her voice widens my smile.

"And Friday—do we forget that happened, too?"

That makes her take a few steps back, the levity between us gone. "Yes. I don't know what I was thinking. I had been drinking and—"

"Don't say that." I push away from the glass. "Don't blame this on the alcohol. You know it had nothing to do with it."

She squares her shoulders. "Yeah, okay, it didn't, but it happened, and I'm over it."

I'm not sure I am, and I don't feel like she is either, but she's shivering, and now I feel like a bigger dick for bringing her out here. Fuck, why can't I think straight?

"Are you done?" she asks.

"Are *we* okay?" I ask.

"*We* aren't anything. I work for you. Friday shouldn't have happened," she expresses with a severity to her tone. I can't help but grimace.

"You don't work for me. My parents were the ones who hired the company you work for."

"Does it matter? I'm still here cleaning your home." She smiles but it doesn't reach her eyes. "Anyway, good luck, and let's work on never running into each other again."

Shooting me in the balls would have felt better than what she just said to me.

Anna goes to walk around me, but I stretch my arm out, stopping her from moving any farther. I'm nothing if not a persistent fuck. "So, what calms your nerves?"

She tips her head up, staring up at me through her lashes. I note the clear contacts shielding the surface of her eyes and how her pupils dilate just a fraction.

Her chest rises, throat bobbing, and she stretches her lips into a sultry smile. Am I seeing that right?

"My fingers." She ducks under my arm and steps back inside, leaving me wondering what she means by that.

It dawns on me a second later.

Oh.

"So I was thinking..." Marc starts, shifting his stick from one hand to the other as we wait in the tunnel.

I always opt for silence before games, which he and everyone on the team knows. It's not a superstitious thing, I just prefer it. *Superstitious* is the cup of tea and peanut butter and jelly sandwich I have before every game while I watch a single episode of *The Punisher*. If I don't do those things, my game is off.

"Not right now." My gaze lands on one of the athletic training students. Her hair is tied in a ponytail. It's not as long or as dark as Anna's, but it's enough to make me think of her.

I told myself I'd stop, but seeing black hair is messing with my head. Because it makes me think of *hers* and how it had been wrapped around my hand. So "not thinking about her" is easier said than done. Her nails dug into me so deep, I not only bled a little, but I have these tiny crescent moon–shaped indentations on my skin.

I was so intoxicated with her presence, I didn't realize how hard she was grabbing on to me until the next day.

I had every intention of forgetting her because I don't mess around with a girl twice, and it seems she feels the same way about guys, or maybe it's just me she doesn't want a repeat of.

She should be long gone from my mind, but she's the reason I came in my jeans from the slightest bit of dry humping.

Damn it to hell. How pathetic.

"Hear me out," he continues even though I'm looking away. "Why don't you ask Anna to bid on you?" His voice is quieter now. "It's obvious she doesn't give a shit about you. She's perfect."

"Ha ha, very funny," I drone out.

"Don't tell me you're actually hurt that she doesn't give a shit about who you are?"

"Hurt? Me? Absolutely not," I retort. "I don't care."

He considers me, eyeing me up and down like he's trying to zero in on my bullshit. "You sound annoyed."

"I'm not, and your idea sounds stupid."

"It's not; it's foolproof. Just think about it. She—and I'm not being funny—doesn't care about who you or your parents are. So it's perfect because she could come bid on you before you two part ways and never speak to each other again. You hate repeats anyway. You're welcome."

"I didn't thank you for anything," I answer, exasperated.

"I just gave you the greatest idea ever. You know I'm right."

Frustratingly enough, he is. Anna already doesn't expect

anything, but I would have to get her to agree first. And I don't see that happening. She's adamant about forgetting I exist.

It'd be great if I could do the same.

"And maybe to entice her to do it, you could pay her…" He trails off. "Just a thought."

I tell myself the only reason I'm entertaining the idea is so she can outbid Florence.

Not because I want to spend time with her.

8

ANNA

"I just don't get why you—" I attempt to swallow, but the thick knot in my throat makes it impossible. Clearing it, I stare out the window, idly dragging my finger along the condensation that's formed on the glass. "Why you can't be supportive?"

Mom called me a few minutes ago to *compromise*, but I know it's to change my mind. I shouldn't have answered, but I held on to hope she would listen. That hasn't happened.

"Stop being so dramatic. I have been supportive. *I am* supportive." She blows out a disgruntled sigh. I can imagine her pinching the bridge of her nose and rolling her eyes. "All I want is the best for you. That's all your father and I have ever wanted. Have you forgotten how hard we've worked? What we did for you and your sister? It's unfair how you're treating us."

"Treating you?" I squeeze my eyes shut, feeling a headache coming on. "All I did was tell you I want to go to culinary school and not law school. We talked about this. You said if I changed my mind, you'd understand."

"Anna." Her tone is passive when she says my name, but I

hear the admonishment. It's the same tone she had when I was a child and she was reprimanding me. "I thought it was something you were saying in the moment. I didn't think you were being serious."

I bite the inside of my cheek hard to stop myself from screaming. "You know how much I love being in the kitchen. You've known—"

"Stop. Just stop. I called you to work things out and instead you're stressing me out. Your father and I have done nothing but be supportive. We let you go to New York even though there are great schools here in North Carolina. We've given you money. We've done so much for you, and this is how you repay us? You ungrateful, selfish girl!"

Tears threaten to spill, but I don't blink. I refuse to cry. "I'm not ungrateful. I've done—"

"Nothing. You've done nothing but be a disappointment. I don't know what we did to deserve this, after everything we sacrificed to come here and give you and Maya a better life. You should learn from your sister. Look at what she's doing. She's going to be a doctor! While you're going to be stuck in a kitchen. A kitchen, for Christ's sake. It isn't reliable or sustainable. You're throwing your future away, and all for what? A job that—"

"You don't have to worry about paying for anything. I can manage. I can—"

"You're damn right you'll be paying." She scoffs so loudly I have to hold the phone away from my ear. "I see that this is going nowhere. You're a lost cause. Useless. When you finally come to your senses and get yourself together, call me and make sure you don't waste my time because you've already done enough of that."

"Mo—" The rest of my words die at the back of my throat as she hangs up.

Dropping my phone on my lap, I ball my hands into tight fists. My temples throb and nausea slithers up my throat, past the lump.

"Anna." Jenny reaches for my hand from the driver's side, and I almost can't stand the careful way she speaks my name. I don't deserve her empathy.

Thank God she's driving the company car, I would have crashed it.

"It's..." My voice breaks but I clear it. "It's fine. I knew this was going to happen. I thought she'd hear me out, but it's fine. I don't want to talk about it anymore." I turn the dial up, letting "Jingle Bell Rock" blast from the van's speakers.

Thankfully, she stays quiet. I shouldn't simmer in Mom's words, but they grow louder by the second, intensifying in my head.

I remind myself to breathe in and out and forge on through a fresh wave of nausea.

A few minutes later we're at Sylas's penthouse. The sickening feeling has somewhat subsided, and my headache has dropped from a seven to a four.

"You'd think with all the money he has, every inch of this place would be decorated. Someone's not very festive. It's giving Scrooge." Jenny grins, jabbing me softly in my side.

I smile a little but falter once I'm standing in the pristine living room. It looks the way it did when we left Monday. It's strange, usually we'll find an empty shaker containing the remnants of a protein shake, his shoes, rolls of cloth tape, jackets and sweaters. But it's spotless, like he's not been here.

I almost let myself believe he's gone for the holidays, but then I hear his heavy footsteps coming down the steps.

"He's here again," she whispers, staring at me, confused. "Did we show up too early? Too late? On the wrong date? This is weird."

I shake my head and agree on the *weird* comment. In the three years we've been cleaning his penthouse, he's *never* been here. Except for a few days ago and now twice this a week.

"Hey," he greets us.

Jenny, of course, smiles cheerily and waves at him, but I'm not sure how to feel. Though I don't know what there is to feel. This is his home, after all. He can be here if he wants. Which he is, obviously, and now flashbacks of Friday play in my head.

Jenny elbows me in the arm, interrupting my thoughts. "Huh?"

"Can I talk to you?" Sylas asks me, the corners of his mouth curling upward into a small smile, making his dimples indent on his cheeks. I notice the slight scruff on his jaw as it flexes every few seconds, like he's chewing on something.

"About?" I've been trying to keep my distance from him since our run-in, and I hoped he'd want to do the same.

"I need to talk to you. It'll be quick. I promise."

"Go." Jenny not-so-gently nudges me.

I give her a look, but she feigns ignorance, grabbing the cart and tugging it along with her to the bathroom.

"*Traidora.*" I glare at her.

Sylas quietly chuckles, and I wonder if he understood me.

We once again find ourselves on the terrace. I expect to be blasted with frosty Manhattan air, wait for the inevitable lingering smell of acrid stale tobacco, but neither happens. I search for the ashtrays and butts that are usually scattered about, but I don't see them either.

It's surprisingly warm and while I catch the faintest whiff of tobacco, there's an overpowering smell of cedar and something expensive. I can't pinpoint what it is, but it's enticing.

"I want to make you a proposition," he begins, jaw flexing harder as he tucks his hands in his pockets, but not before I notice the tremors.

"Are you okay?" I eye him, skeptical and a little concerned.

"Yeah, why?" He chews faster.

"You look like you're about to have a heart attack or something," I joke, but he looks visibly uncomfortable, so I tone it down. "No, really, are you okay?"

He flashes me a grin that manifests into a smug smirk. "Cute. You're worried about me."

This is what I get for showing concern. "No, calling 9-1-1 would be a nightmare and I have another job to be at. I'm not trying to be here all day."

"And here I thought you cared." He pops a bubble and for some odd reason unbeknownst to me, it's kind of...hot.

My headache is now at a two, and surprisingly, I feel calmer despite the conversation with my mother. "Seriously, are you okay?"

He ruffles a hand through his mussed hair, the tremor slight but not as bad as when I first noticed it. "Yeah, just trying out a new thing. Hadn't realized how hard going cold turkey would be. It's a bitch, I'll tell you that."

He's not insinuating what I think he is...Is he? "You stopped smoking?"

Sylas shrugs. "A bratty smartass said it wasn't good for my health, so I'm trying gum. Seeing what all the rave is about."

I don't mean to, but I can't stop my lips from lifting upward. "She's not bratty, she's smart as fuck."

"Let me guess? Graduated top ten in your class or something?"

"Number one," I correct proudly.

"Valedictorian twins."

"You graduated top of your class? Did Daddy pay for that too?" Okay, that was a bitchy thing to say, but after knowing his dad paid for him to pass our communications class, I can't help but wonder.

He laughs, full and deep. "Sadly, no, daddy dearest didn't pay my way to becoming valedictorian in high school. Freshman year of college, on the other hand, he was feeling rather...*guilty*." His pale green eyes harden, face grim and taut as if he were remembering something, but then he does a one-eighty and his smile and posture become lax. "I happen to be very smart."

While I'm tempted to ask what that was, I don't.

"Right, it really shows," I drawl, to which he chuckles. "So, gum..."

I didn't anticipate for my words to hold any weight. I had expected him to blow me off.

"It's all the rave." He's between serious and sarcastic, I can't tell which, but I smile either way. "Right, then. Proposition. I want to make one."

I narrow my eyes. "With me?"

"Yeah, I'll get straight to the point. There's an auction on Friday I have to be part of. If you have nothing to do, I'd like for you to attend. I'll give you the money to bid on me and that's all you'll have to do. *When* you win, we'll part ways and you'll never have to worry about me bothering you again."

I blink, feeling both amused and perplexed. I know about these auctions and how much money goes into them. Never been to one as I'm too broke to attend one.

"Me? Why?"

"Because you don't give a fuck about who I am."

"And because I won't expect a date?"

"Mhm. So what do you say? I'll pay you."

I don't know whether to be annoyed or ask how much. "What do I look like? Just because we—"

"You need the money. I overhead you Monday and, well...I'll give you ten grand."

If they could, my eyes would pop out of their sockets. I jolt back and blink rapidly, still not able to process his words. "You'd give me ten grand, just like that?"

"Just like that," he says simply.

This isn't real. It can't be, right? This has to be a prank.

"Don't worry about it. I'll find someone else to do it." That disrupts my thoughts and cuts through the silence.

He turns, but I stop him. "No, wait, don't do that." I grab the crook of his elbow. "I'll be there. Just tell me what I need to wear, where it'll be at, and what time."

It's so desperate and I hate myself for it, but I'll admonish myself later. I'd be stupid to turn down ten grand.

He looks smug, and I realize he wanted me desperate. Fucking asshole. "I'll give you my number and send you the details."

"*Pendejo*," I mutter, drawing out my phone from my pocket.

"*A veces.*" He winks at me.

So, he does understand Spanish. Oh.

Friday, December 13

"It seems too good to be true!" I yell from my bedroom as I hook my earring on my left lobe.

"I get it..." Jenny hums pensively and grows quiet, letting Shakira's voice filter throughout our apartment.

I hum along to "Rabiosa," hoping it'll help drown out my thoughts, but they're too loud, overriding the lyrics.

It's been two days since Sylas and I came to an agreement and two days since we last talked to each other. After he gave me his number, he sent me the e-invite with dress code details, let me know I could bring a plus-one, and then ran me through how the auction would play out.

I'm not usually a person who likes to mull over my thoughts, but I'm still waiting for the *I don't need you anymore* text or to show up to an abandoned warehouse where the silver spoons will sacrifice my body.

That last one seems unlikely, but I've been around the rich for three years. I know what they get up to. Been to a few parties in their extravagant homes. I've not *seen* them do any crazy rituals, but that doesn't mean they haven't.

"Do you think I'm making a mistake?" I step out of my bedroom, my mocha-brown heels clicking with every step.

Jenny turns to look at me before she turns back and does a

double take. "Holy shit, Anna." Her jaw goes slack, eyes doubling in size. "That dress was made for you."

Thanks to Jenny, I was able to borrow an olive-green satin gown from Saks Fifth Avenue. It has an open back, a cowl neck, and a long slit down my thigh. It's the prettiest, most expensive thing I've ever worn.

And I say "borrow" because Jenny begged her manager to let us use it for the event. She agreed, so long as we return it as-new first thing tomorrow.

It came with a price though. Jenny has to pick up extra shifts this month because of how busy they are, starting tonight. Which really sucks because she was going to be my plus-one. Now I have to go alone. And if the dress is damaged in any way, it'll be coming out of Jenny's paycheck.

But I assured them both that wouldn't happen. I also told Jenny I'd be splitting Sylas's money with her. It's only fair since she's having to pick up extra shifts because of me. She protested, but I'm going to do it anyway.

I smile as I twirl for her. "You don't think this is too much, do you?"

It's not that I don't feel good in the dress, because I really do. I know I look good, but it's a black-tie event. There's a high slit and it's snug on me.

"No, you look hot as fuck." She whistles and does a circle motion with her finger. I twirl again and smile until it hurts when she pulls her phone out and starts snapping pictures. "You're making me reconsider whether dicks are worth it."

I smile before my lips fall in a flat line. "Okay, in all serious-ness...don't you think this is weird?"

I know the auction is real, but Sylas wanting *me* to help him sounds unreal.

She sets her phone down and stands in front of me, placing her hands on my shoulders. "In the spirit of the holidays, I'm choosing to believe this is some Christmas miracle. Or that some-one's watching out for you." She shrugs and drops her hands.

"Don't get me wrong, it is strange and I don't get it, but he's rich. So, I guess let's not question it. But if things get weird, you call me. I'll hop in a Lyft and take care of him."

She grabs a pencil from the counter and uses it to stab the air.

I laugh. "Okay, John Wick, chill out. If anything happens, I'll call you and I'll leave immediately. But is it strange that I trust him while also feeling off about the entire situation?"

Jenny shakes her head. "No, I get it. I'd feel weird about it too. But hey, you must have some kind of magical pussy powers if he wants you."

I cringe, scrunching my nose. "Ew, never say that again."

"Just saying. You've also got a fan-fucking-tastic ass…You really are making me question my sexuality."

I roll my eyes but smile. "Have a good shift. I'll text you when I'm out."

"Thanks for taking one for the team." She blows me a kiss.

I hate that Jenny isn't here.

The auction hasn't started, so guests are socializing, looking at the art displayed on the walls, and enjoying the live band playing Christmas music.

I'm in the restroom, staring at my reflection in the full-length mirror. I've been here for a few minutes and have every intention of staying here until the auction begins. I feel supremely out of place.

While I could sit at my designated table and fake that I'm having a good time schmoozing with the rich, I don't have it in me to pretend.

"Your dress is gorgeous. Is that a Kim Liu?" an older lady asks as she washes her hands.

I glance down at my dress, not having the slightest clue who the designer is. "Uh...yeah. It's a Kim Liu."

She dries her hand and gives me a once-over. "I thought so. You look amazing."

"Thanks." I smile at her. "So do you."

She mirrors my smile. "Thanks. Happy bidding."

That'll probably be the highlight of my night because I can't imagine it getting any better.

I don't look toward the door when I hear it swing open. I'm pretending to fix my bun in the mirror when I hear the soft snick of the lock.

I glance over and jerk back a little, stunned.

Sylas is in the restroom. And he looks...*good* in his tux.

It molds to his body in a way that leaves no doubt in my mind it's custom made. It frames and outlines his broad shoulders, long torso, and thick thighs, and his usually mussed hair is slicked back.

Wow.

"Wow." He exhales a breath.

I blink out of the trance, realizing I'm gaping and haven't said a word.

My cheeks burn a little. "You know, this is the women's restroom. The men's is just down the hall."

His gaze works slowly down my body, stopping at the slit in my dress. His throat bobs around a thick swallow before he darts his attention back up. "Wow."

My heart stutters. "You already said that."

His lips part then close before they part again. "Yeah...I'm... you left me speechless."

Same.

Now my heart stops working. I've never had anyone say that to me before. My cheeks blister and my stomach whirls with... butterflies. "Wh-what are you doing in here?"

"You've been here for a while. I was waiting, but the auction is about to begin, and I wanted to talk to you before it started."

I lift a brow. "What's so important you couldn't wait and had to lock us in here?"

"Just wanted to make sure you got the money."

My brow furrows. "I thought I texted you I did?"

He rubs the nape of his neck. "I wanted a verbal confirmation."

I take one step closer and so does he, until we're standing an arm's length from one another. "I got it. Is that verbal enough?"

"Yeah." Sylas licks his lips.

My gaze lingers on his mouth and I suck in a breath, shifting away. "So, what are you still doing here?"

"Doing what you're doing." He tucks his hand in his pockets, gaze drifting down the dress again.

"And what's that?"

"Hiding."

"I'm not—" His knowing look shuts me up, so I shrug. "And if I am? I don't know anyone. I don't fit in with the people out there." I don't voice that out of pity, but we both know it's true. I'm here out of desperation because I need money; I don't know what his excuse is. "Why are you here?"

"I hate these things." He tugs on the collar of his button-down. "Kissing the asses of people who don't give a single shit about me but only care who my parents are is a lot of fun," he remarks dryly.

Sylas's sarcastic response baffles me. Nothing about it sounds disingenuous. "If it makes you feel any better, I don't give a shit about you or your parents."

That has him smiling, and I don't know why but it makes me feel good. "You really didn't look me up?"

"Why would I want to do that?"

"I'm a very interesting person."

I laugh, taking another step forward as he does. "Mmm, who lied to you?"

"You seemed to think so when I was making you feel *really* good the other night."

My heels click as I shift on my feet. "You got me off. That doesn't make you interesting."

His finger brushes my forearm, simultaneously freezing and burning me. "I could show you just how interesting I really am."

Sylas removes his finger and from the corner of my eye, I see it suspended in the air, next to my arm, like he's waiting for something. "I'm sorry."

"For what?" I'm breathless and hot.

"I didn't ask if I could touch you." His eyes turn molten as they rake over me again.

My lips tick up. "Ask me and make it sound desperate."

I don't know what we're doing or why I like this so much, but I can't bring myself to question it.

He leans down, his lips close to the ear, minty breath fanning it. "Can I touch you? Please let me touch you. I need to feel you, Anna."

The desperation in his voice really throws me off. I asked him to make it sound like it but didn't anticipate the genuine desire, the yearn raw in his voice, the searing look in his eyes.

"Do it." I swallow hard.

Sylas clutches my hip, fingers digging deep, but the moment is short-lived because someone pounds on the door.

"Sy, it's about to start. Hurry the fuck up."

Our eyes collide and breaths tangle, heat and electricity wrapping around us. We don't part even as the voice outside reminds him that he can't be late.

"Whatever happens out there, you don't stop bidding on me," he all but pleads, effectively reminding me why I'm here.

I bid, he pays me, and then we part ways.

Stepping away from him, I give a mock salute. "Don't worry. 'Tis the season to be bidding."

The girls and their parents have gone wild.

I just witnessed the captain of the basketball team, Lucas Calloway, get auctioned off for seven thousand eight hundred dollars. And his teammate before him went for six grand.

When Sylas first gave me the money, I thought ten thousand was a ridiculous sum. I thought to myself, *who would bid that much money on a guy? He isn't even a pro.* But it's my fault for underestimating the power of money, influence, and good looks.

Now I'm worried ten grand won't be enough.

"All right, ladies and gentlemen, up next we have Sylas Lenoir Alves," the auctioneer announces after Lucas steps off the stage. Sylas takes his place, a flirtatious grin on display, dimples indented deep on each cheek. My body buzzes and heart thunders as I remember how he touched me, how he looked at me, how his voice deepened.

His eyes immediately find mine and lock in. My stomach dips, heart thrashing like it's begging to be let out. I don't know why, since we don't know each other well enough for me to be into him. An orgasm or two shouldn't change anything—I've done casual before, but I feel...infatuated, and I don't know how to make that stop. We've not known each other long. Just a few days I couldn't stand him and now—this can't be happening.

I smile a little at him and his own only widens; his eyes are still on me, but we both snap out of it when the auctioneer starts the bid at one thousand.

All over the room, paddles are raised high. I'm so stunned by the number of people who want to spend a day with him that I forget to raise my paddle.

Right, I'm bidding. I quickly raise mine and continue to do so as the auctioneer shouts increasingly higher numbers.

I get a little nervous once we approach eight thousand. A hot blonde and me are the only ones left. If I'm not mistaken, she was with Sylas at dinner a few days ago. It doesn't seem like she's going to give up, but I see the waver on her face when the auctioneer calls, "Eight thousand five hundred," like she's not sure if she should keep going.

A look of trepidation crosses Sylas's face, like he's worried the hot blonde is going to win.

I wonder if he knew she'd bid on him and that she'd be persistent about it. He begged me not to stop bidding though, and I promised I wouldn't.

There's a thousand dollars in my bank account along with what he sent. That'd make eleven thousand. I'm either about to make the best or worst decision of the night.

Fuck it.

"Eleven thousand!" I shout.

I'm not sure if I'm allowed to do that, but it's too late to retract my offer.

The auctioneer's eyebrows skyrocket and his lips split into a wide grin. "Whoa, we're past ten thousand for the first time tonight!" He chuckles and so do the people around me. "Eleven thousand! Can we make that eleven thousand one hundred?" He looks at the blonde.

Sylas's eyes widen with worry for a second before they relax when she shakes her head.

"Going once..." He pauses to give her or anyone else a chance. "Going twice..." Another pause. "Well, okay then. Sold to the lovely lady in green!"

The auctioneer goes on to remind me and everyone else in the room what Sylas has planned for us, but I've already checked out. I know the date isn't going to happen, so there's no point in listening. Still, I smile like I'm the luckiest girl in the world, hold his stare that says I'm the only one he has eyes for, and take a good look at him before we never see each other again.

9

SYLAS

"HOLY SHIT," MARC WHISPER-YELLS AS I COME OFF THE stage and Frost takes my place.

I feel just as dumbfounded as he looks. I only gave Anna ten thousand, which means she willingly used her own money to bid on me. I didn't ask her to do that, and I wouldn't have been upset if she backed down because Florence is relentless. But Anna matched her energy, had this determined look on her face like she refused to lose.

"Biggest clutch of the year," he says, astonished. "So, that's it, then?"

I look around, making sure the other guys aren't listening. "Yeah. We said once she bid, that'd be it for us."

His black brows knit, gaze searching my face. "Why do you look disappointed?"

Do I? Am I?

No. What am I thinking? I'm not disappointed, it's whatever. It's done.

"I-I..." Did I just stutter? "I'm not."

"Right," he drawls, chuckling.

"I really—"

"Sy." Alexander Van Doren, King's Yard's star quarterback, drapes an arm around my shoulder and quietly asks, "So, who is she?"

I keep a smile on my face, but it feels too tight at the suggestion in his voice. "Don't worry about it."

He scoffs, side-eyeing me. "Don't be like that. You've never been shy about sharing. What's her name?"

I bite my tongue, resisting the urge to tell him to fuck off. I only smile wider and pat his chest. "She's not interested."

"Did she tell you that?" He lifts a challenging brow.

"I—" I falter. Why am I cockblocking Anna? She could be interested. Alex isn't bad looking, and he's a decent guy in general. But fuck that, I'm better looking and I'm not just decent, I'm great. "She didn't but she came here with *me*, so back the fuck up and stay in your lane."

Marc's lips twitch at the corners, eyes twinkling with amusement, but he keeps his mouth shut.

He huffs a laugh, dropping his arm and pulling away. "Stay in my lane because she's taken, or stay in my lane because she's *going to be* taken?"

Jesus Christ. "Does it matter?"

Alex smirks cunningly. "I'm going to take that as not taken."

I don't manage to get a word in because he walks away.

"I thought you didn't care if you never talked to her again?" Marc muffles his snicker.

"Shut up." I swallow back a groan, doing my best to ignore the frustration mounting in my chest. "Maybe I do, but we had an agreement."

He stares at me like he's not following, and his words say just as much. "Okay and? You're nothing if not a persistent asshole. Go talk to her."

"And then what?"

I have no idea where to go from there. I've never gone back for seconds with a girl and I shouldn't assume she even wants me. Sure, the moment in the restroom was lovely and even more so because it was with her, but it wasn't long enough to mean anything, right? Or did it mean something?

My heart did that wild thing, and my mind was kind of all over the place. That never happens, but the moment I saw her, despite how scattered my thoughts were, I went to this happy place. I can't explain it and it's weird because I don't know her, but it feels like I do.

He shrugs. "The hell if I know, but go for it or someone else will."

Fuck it, I will.

"I'll see you later," I say over my shoulder.

I take a peek where everyone is sitting, but I don't see her and assume she went to pay, so that's where I head. By the time I manage to extricate myself from the crowd, the person taking the donations tells me she already paid.

She couldn't have already left. She's probably outside waiting for her ride. I offered to pick her up, but she said she had it handled.

Just as I'm about to go check Mom blocks my path.

"Sylas, sweetheart." She smiles primly, but it's strained like the rest of her face. She runs a palm down the lapels of my tux, smoothing them out. "We need to talk."

"I really can't right now. I need to go." I flash her my best smile, hoping it doesn't look as fake as this entire interaction is.

I love her and I know in her own way she loves me, but she's more concerned about appearances and all that bullshit. Which is why she's retouching my bow tie, smiling like a mother should.

"I'll make it quick." She drops her hand just as Dad takes his place by her side. "Who is she?"

"She's..." I stagger, my gaze landing on Florence as she comes to stand next to my mother.

What is she doing here? God, she's everywhere.

"I really thought I had a chance at winning." She sighs, her disappointment evident.

I did too and was kind of shocked she didn't keep bidding, but whatever.

"Don't worry about it, Florence. I'm sure we can figure something out. Can't we, Sylas?" Mom shoots me a threatening look. "Maybe the girl and you can switch, she can go out with Frost."

Frost? Did Florence bid on Everett? I thought she hated him. He dislikes her just as much.

"But she—"

"Just tell the girl there's been a change of plans," Dad interjects, sounding uninterested. "She'll understand."

I fist my hand as a tremor runs through my fingers. I want to smoke, but I threw my cigarettes away. My breath picks up, chest tight and compressed like something is sitting on it. I tell myself to breathe, to think.

"I can't do that because she's my girl...friend." I can't believe that came out of my mouth. Their faces recoil in shock... betrayal...disgust. I'm not sure, but for the first time in my life, I've stunned them into silence.

I'm just as surprised. I didn't mean to say that and I shouldn't have, but I didn't know what else to say. I can't take it back now.

"And we're meeting up now and going out. So, if you'll excuse me..." I do the cowardly thing and bolt before they can ask questions.

I stop in my tracks when I spot her by the entrance and see she's not alone. She's with Alex, and she's smiling big at him. My stomach knots, and I have to fist my hands at my side again. Force my feet not to move to her and make an ass of myself.

When she laughs at whatever he said, I make the decision to turn and walk away but don't make it far when she calls my name.

"Sylas." She says it like she's both relieved and happy to see me and her face exudes that when I spin and our eyes connect. An electric current rushes through my body, making it thrum vigorously. "Where are you going? Are we not leaving?"

I recover and stroll over to them. "Yeah, sorry, I thought I left my phone, but it's right here." I pat my pocket. "I'm ready to go. You weren't waiting long, were you?" I stand next to her and don't give it a second thought as I slip my arm around her back, pin her side to mine, and lay my palm on top of her hip.

She grins up at me and I note a charged glint in her eyes that makes my heart race. "Not long." Her body is pliant against mine. I don't want to put too much thought into this, but she so easily and comfortably lets me hold her. She feels right next to me. It's strange, but what's stranger is how much I like it.

I look back at Alex, dimming my smile into something casual, making sure it doesn't look smug.

His eyes track the movement then his lips pinch in a tight smile. "Got it. I'll stay in my lane."

"You do that." I give him a dismissive once-over.

"I'll see you, Anna." He tips his head at me then pivots and walks away.

We watch him leave, neither one of us moving, and even when we know he's gone, we don't shift. I know I should let go and I think she's thinking it too, but we stay as we are.

"Thanks for playing along. He wouldn't get the hint." A relieved sigh slips past her lips.

"Are you okay?"

"Yeah." Her gaze traces over my concerned expression then glances down at my hand where I'm holding her a little tighter than I mean to. "I'm seriously okay. He didn't do anything but continue in many different ways to ask me out."

"Sorry about that." I force myself to let her go and add a bit of distance between us. But that only forces my gaze to gravitate to her dress and how it frames her body in a way that makes it look painted on. The way I felt when I first saw her is the same way I feel now: speechless, for lack of a better word. "I—"

I can't draw up a word perfect enough to describe just how divine she looks. "Beautiful" would be doing her a disservice. I'm stumped and annoyed I can't think of something better.

"You what?"

"You look beautiful, Anna."

"Oh." Her face brightens, smile tender and breathtaking, and pink blooms on her cheeks. "Thanks. It was fun to dress up. I can't remember the last time I went all out like this."

I do a little bow and when I lift my head, we lean into each other, chuckling. "Glad I could be of service."

She looks over her shoulder at the exit and then at her phone. "Thanks again for playing along." She pauses like she's contemplating something, her eyes roaming over me. "My Lyft will be here soon, so you don't have to stick around. I'm sure Alexander's not going to show up."

"Yeah..." Now I look over mine, back to where the auction is still taking place. "Thanks again for doing this for me. You were great out there."

"I hate losing although the blonde winning wouldn't have been the worst thing in the world. She's gorgeous. Is she why you wanted me to keep bidding?"

I nod. "Our parents are best friends. They're convinced we'll get married and have"—I shudder—"babies."

She winces. "Yikes."

"I know."

"Look on the bright side. She's hot, so your babies will be gorgeous."

I laugh. "Please don't say that. I don't need or want that kind of negative energy."

"You don't want kids?"

"Not right now. Maybe in ten or fifteen years, but definitely not with her." I glower at the thought of being tied to Florence in that way.

"Well, you're welcome. I just saved you from marriage and

babies." She laughs and I swear it's the prettiest thing I've ever heard.

But speaking of Florence... *Anna is going to hate me.* "I need to tell you something."

"Oh good, we caught you before you left." My parents saunter over toward us looking regal and commanding.

My spine stiffens and I glance at Anna. *She's definitely going to hate me.*

"Hi, I'm Anna." She plasters a faux friendly, all-business smile —the same one from the restaurant. "It's so good to meet you."

"Yes, it's so good to meet my son's girlfriend." Dad scrutinizes her. "I can't believe we didn't know about you until now." It's so belittling, I know Anna feels it.

Fuck my life. Why didn't I start off with that first?

I look at Anna, but she's not looking at me. She's staring at them with an indiscernible expression.

"Wait." Mom eyes her up and down with all the judgment in the world. "You're that waitress from Clover's and our...housekeeper." The disdain in her voice seals it, and I just want to fucking crawl in a hole.

I prepare for the worst. My fingers tremble and become sweaty, and my pulse goes haywire, threatening to explode.

"I am," Anna says, keeping the practiced friendliness intact. *Why did I lie?* "I'm so sorry we've kept our relationship from you." That renders me speechless, but her slipping her warm hand in mine makes my mind go blank. When she rests her head on my shoulder, I lose all sense of existence. "It's actually brand new." She squeezes my hand, nails digging into the skin like she's trying to pull me back to reality, like she knows I'm lost in my head. "We're taking things slow. Still getting to know one another."

"Yes, slow. We're just taking it slow." My voice comes out robotic.

She squeezes my hand again, harder this time.

I need a cigarette—no, a whole damn pack.

Mom and Dad's gazes bounce between us, still not believing

what they're hearing or seeing, but then they pull themselves together.

And I do too. My erratic nervous system calms as she brushes the pad of her thumb on the crook between my thumb and index finger.

Mom isn't buying it. Her gaze drops to our hands, and she sneers. "But you didn't say a thing to him at the restaurant. Or to us. You—"

"I was working, and despite how much I like your son, I wanted to maintain professionalism." She answers steadily and without missing a beat, lying so smoothly even I believe her for a second.

When she tips her head up and our eyes lock, I breathe easier.

"And I didn't want Anna to get in trouble." I lean down, kissing the crown of her head. That's probably pushing it, but how else would I sell it? I don't think they're buying it, but they don't look as distrusting as they did a moment ago.

"Hmm..." Dad doesn't say anything, doesn't even look at her anymore.

"Now that you've all met, we have to get going. We're going out to dinner. I'll see you later."

"It was so good to meet you both." She extends her palm, and they begrudgingly shake it.

I'm ushering Anna outside, hand in hand, before they can change their minds and continue to interrogate us.

The arctic air is a relief to my burning lungs. I inhale deeply, despite the frost that feels like it's impaling my skin. I pat the inside of my jack—*right, no cigarettes*—but I do find a pack of gum and pop three pieces in my mouth.

"I'm sorry. I didn't mean to put you on the spot or to lie but—"

"Are we still grabbing dinner?" she asks, her expression oddly empathetic.

"Is this a trick question where you proceed to slap the shit out of me for—"

She bursts out a laugh. "I don't like solving my problems by throwing hands. I mean, is the temptation there? Yeah. But I don't want to hit you. I do want to eat though. I'm starving."

I'm so lucky it was her. I'm so lucky she's here.

"Yeah, I know a place." I hold out my hand, not totally sure why. She stares at it, and I wonder whether she'll leave it floating, but she takes it.

10

ANNA

WE STAND IN FRONT OF A SMALL BUILDING. A BRIGHT-red neon sign above the door says *Strangers* with a person on either side of it, their arms stretched under the word as if they're holding it while they shake hands.

"You brought me to a dive bar?" I hold my jacket tighter to my body.

I don't care that we're here. I'm actually excited. Places like this always have the best food. But we're so overdressed, and I have to return this dress as I got it.

"I hope that's okay? I swear they have the best burgers here."

My stomach grumbles and mouth waters, but the thought of getting this dress dirty stops me. I will have the money to pay it off now, but I'm trying to save it for important things like bills and getting a new mixer.

"This is more than okay. I love burgers but..." I shouldn't be, but I'm a bit embarrassed to admit that I don't own this dress. I also don't want his pity. "Should we not get changed? We're so overdressed and—"

"I'm going to be honest with you right now." He cuts me off.

"I would hope you're honest with me all the time." We exchange a smile that makes my stomach dip and flutter.

"I am, but right now, I'm going to be extra honest," he says, and I snicker but don't comment. "I feel like I didn't get to appreciate you in the dress long enough. It's not fair that you got to be around so many people and they had the chance to see you in it all night, to sit next to you. It's not fair and I'm not sorry when I say I'm going to be selfish because I want my time now with you while you're wearing this dress."

My smile slips, heart racing. The heavy thud feels like it's at my ear, drowning out all other sounds.

Thank God it's dark out or he'd see how fiercely my face is burning. I don't know what I thought he was going to say but it wasn't that.

I expel a shuddering breath, hating what I'm about to admit. "We really can't go in there. This dress isn't mine. I have to return it first thing tomorrow morning. But we can take a picture and—"

"How much was it?"

"No, don't do that." I shake my head.

"No, *you* don't do that." He inches a little closer to me. "We're already here, I'm hungry, and you are too." I'm starving. I didn't eat much before, and at the auction, they only served finger foods. "And I should be paying for your dress. After all, you went out of your way to do me a favor. So, this and anything else that you paid for is on me. Add in the fact I lied to my parents, it's the least I can do. I'm sorry I didn't consider it first."

Sylas genuinely sounds apologetic, but the stubborn part of my brain is urging me to refuse. However, my pride diminishes at his next words.

"I'm not trying to be that person, but you know I have more than enough money. If that still doesn't sit right with you, just remember I used you the other night and today. Now you have to use me back. And please do. I really want you to use me." He's closer than before, and our breath clouds together, becoming one, before mine dwindles as he raises his hand to my cold cheek. Like the other night, he pushes a strand of hair away from my face, placing it back with the rest. "I'm okay with being used by you, but if you don't like the word *used*, we can just call it one friend helping another."

We're friends now? It's at the tip of my tongue, but I don't ask. Things could change tomorrow; he could act like he doesn't know me, or he could surprise me and prove that I misjudged him. Even though I shouldn't, I'm hoping for the latter. Either way, I let it be and accept what he's willing to give me. I'd be stupid to turn all of this down.

"No, I like *used* better. It's only fair." It's really not the same thing, but then again, it sort of is? I don't know, but it doesn't matter. I'm not going to think about us using each other because I *definitely* don't want him to use me again. But will I be thinking about it? Yeah...

He notes my shudder and places his hand on the small of my back, escorting me inside.

"It is, isn't it?" His dimples dent his cheeks as he holds the door open for me.

Inside, warmth quickly envelops me, and I stop shivering almost immediately. We get glanced at, but it's quick and fleeting. Everyone is in their own world, drinking, playing pool or darts, dancing, singing karaoke, or using the pinball or claw machines.

Sylas guides me fluidly through the crowd, hand still firmly planted at my back. Every so often, I feel him stroke me, his touch hovering above my butt. I don't mean to, but I hold my breath when it happens because, embarrassingly, I'm hoping he touches me.

I shift my focus away from his hand to our surroundings in hopes it'll distract me. Different-colored Christmas lights hang from the ceilings, along with signed picture frames of bands, license plates from different states, vinyl cases, and in a corner, a large disco ball. On the walls, there's more pictures of musicians, different sports jerseys from King's Yard, and a few scattered Christmas decorations. The chairs and tables are all mismatched and look like they were picked up off the side of the road.

It's chaotic, bright, and right up my alley.

We walk farther until we find a red high-top table, nestled in the corner right underneath the disco ball. The table and chairs sparkle from the lights reflecting off the mirrors on the ball.

I don't need it, but Sylas helps me onto the chair, and when I fold one leg over the other, his gaze drops to the slit as it widens. He sucks his lip between his teeth, smothering a chuckle as he sits and scoots his chair closer to mine.

I make no comment because I know he's just as hyperaware as I am about the sexual tension choking us. I'm not going to pretend I don't want him, but one time was enough. I don't want to get carried away and somehow find myself getting attached because strangely enough, I can see it happening.

And I'm going to go out on a limb and assume he's being this friendly because I lied to his parents. I knew something was off the moment they showed up and his demeanor changed.

I did the only thing I could think of: lie. I don't know how much they believed us, but I think I did okay, and I hope he's feeling better. He seems like it, considering he's been more talkative and his usual arrogant self.

He gives me a rundown of the menu, and when I tell him what I want to eat and drink, he leaves. While he's gone, I take my jacket off, but despite Sylas being gone for a while, I can't seem to cool down.

It doesn't help that as he retakes his seat, I see he's pulled off his bow tie. The first two buttons are undone on his shirt, and it looks like he ran his fingers through his hair. It's disheveled but in a good way. On top of all of that, he smells amazing.

He hands me my bottle of beer and clinks the neck with his. "Cheers to being used."

"Cheers." I laugh and take a swig.

"Don't think I've forgotten. How much was it and how much

did you pay for your Lyft?" He rests his arm along the back of my chair, the tips of his finger gently brushing against my skin.

For a couple of *friends*, we're huddled mighty close to each other. I should push him away, but I welcome his touch, ignoring the protest in my head. My brain is screaming to back away, to stop whatever it is I'm doing, but my body revels in how it feels to be wrapped in him. I also can't stop staring at how his pants strain against his thick thighs and his button-down clings to his stomach, faintly outlining his abs.

Technically, we're fake dating, so I'm not doing anything wrong.

When I tell him the price, he fishes out his phone from his pocket and goes to his banking app. I look away because while I'm curious about his finances, I'd rather not know and get jealous. So what? Sue me.

"I've sent it as well as everything I owed you." He sets his phone down and I feel mine vibrate seconds later.

"You really didn't need to do that, but thanks."

"I wanted to, and why not?" He takes a swig of his beer, staring intently at me.

"I don't want to seem ungrateful, but it's not like I'll wear this dress again."

"You could for me." He smirks.

"And then what would we do?" I lean forward, moving away from his touch. It's making me dizzy, or that could be the beer with how little I've eaten today.

"Stuff," he replies.

I grin. "You have no idea, do you?"

He chuckles. "Not a clue. Can you tell?"

"It's okay. I don't either. I'm not a dater, so I wouldn't know." It's the truth. While I've messed around, I've never had a boyfriend. There was that one time in high school, but it wasn't long enough to be considered serious. "I promise, I'm not judging."

Sylas leans forward, resting his elbow on the table. It grazes mine, and I'm tempted to move because my brain feels foggy from his touch, but I remain in place.

"Really?" He sounds invested in that tidbit. "You don't do boyfriends?"

I scrunch my nose and shake my head. "No. Mainly because I came here on scholarship, so my goal was to get good grades, get into law school, and get out. I also wanted the full college experience, and having a boyfriend would prevent that."

I'm not embarrassed to admit that. I like having sex and I know Sylas does too.

There's no judgment, but interest piques his face. "The goal *was*?" I take a large swig of my beer and then another. "Did I hit a nerve? That wasn't my intention."

"It's nothing."

"We have all night." He flashes me a small smile, and my stare lingers on his cheeks, hoping his dimples will reappear. "And it'll be a bit until they bring out the food. I also asked them to keep the drinks coming. Come on, share, then I'll share something with you."

I perk up. "You're going to share something with me?"

"That's what friends do, don't they?" His leg brushes up against mine, and again my brain sends a signal to my lower half to move. I don't.

"It's nothing interesting. It's actually really stupid." I spin my bottle on the tabletop, scowling a little at the reminder.

"I'm all ears. You have me all night, for as long as you want."

I've never smiled this big. *What is he doing to me?*

I sit back, finally adding space between us. "Don't feel bad for me, okay?"

He raises his right hand. "No pity. Got it."

Huffing a breath, I rehash my family drama. "My parents have always wanted me to be a lawyer, and for a while I wanted that too. But I've also always liked cooking and baking, but I never really thought anything of it. Mainly because my parents said it was a stupid dream. That it would lead to an 'unreliable job.'" I hold my hands up to make air quotes, using the break to consider my next words. "I listened because they immigrated to this country for a better life and wanted my sister and me to have that, too. Who was I to argue with that? But...I don't know...somewhere along the way, I found a bigger love for food and started coming up with my own recipes. Anyway, after a lot of back-and-forth, I decided to scratch becoming a lawyer and attempt culinary school. I spoke to my parents, hoping they'd hear me out, but they didn't. They said they weren't going to watch me throw my life away. So, I had to pick between law or culinary. I picked the latter and now they've cut me off."

I take a pull of my beer, relishing the bitter tang over the taste of the words that left my mouth.

A muscle on his jaw works, but he says nothing.

"Hey." I wave my hand in front of his face. "No feeling bad for me. I knew what would happen. It is what it is."

My stomach sinks at the thought that this will be my first Christmas without them. I could still go see my other family members, but it'd be weird, and I don't want to ruin the holidays for everyone else.

Sylas looks like he wants to speak, but he just blinks and offers me a lopsided grin. A worker comes by and sets a large pitcher on the table with two cups.

We finish off our bottles, and he picks up the pitcher, filling the cups almost to the brim.

"What's in this?" I peer at the red liquid then inhale. My brows arch at the strong scent of tequila.

"I don't know. It's called a 'Christmas Miracle.'"

I snort and clink my glass against his. "Cheers to that."

His face brightens, and right as he's about to take a sip, he pulls his glass away. "And for parental issues. I love that for us."

I take a small sip and recoil, squeezing my eyes shut as the liquid burns and settles in my stomach. "Holy shit."

His eyes flutter, shoulders going taut. "Jesus, someone's

heavy-handed." Despite that, he still proceeds to take another long drink.

"It's your turn to share your *parental issues* with me." I laugh a little, taking small sips of my drink until I'm able to tolerate it.

He slouches back and drags his fingers through his hair.

"Don't tell me you're regretting it? Come on." I poke his side, in awe of how hard it is. "I told you. Now you have to tell me."

"It's really nothing."

I give him a deadpan look. "I'm not going to judge." I poke him again. *Wow, he's firm* all *over.* "It must be bad if you had to lie to them and tell them I'm your girlfriend."

Sylas goes stiff then exhales a ragged breath. "I'm sorry about that." He takes a drink, followed by another. "My parents are... domineering." He drags his tongue along his teeth. "The girl I told you about, at the auction..."

"The blonde?"

He nods. "Florence. They *really* want us to happen."

"Is this a keeping-it-in-the-circle kind of thing?" I say to lighten the mood.

His lips jerk up a smidge. "Something like that."

"The whole *we hate you* look makes sense now," I quip.

"I'm sorry. Again. They're—"

I wave a hand. "It's okay. I'm not offended. I work at Clover's"—it's the kind of expensive, by-reservation-only restaurant celebrities dine at—"and I'm a housekeeper. I've seen and heard it all. I'm really fine, but are *you* okay?"

He looked like he was struggling for air, like he was close to a panic attack. I hated knowing he was feeling that way and his parents were to blame.

I would know; my parents bring out the worst in me.

"Oh me? Yeah, I'm good." He grins, all boyish and ambivalent. "They stress me out a bit, but I'm used to it. I was mostly worked up because, you know, I'm not smoking anymore, so the change is different."

While I believe the nicotine withdrawal might've been the reason behind the way he acted, I know it's not the sole reason.

"I'm sorry." The words are out and my hand is on his forearm before I can stop myself.

"Hey, no pity. Remember?" Sylas pierces me with a look. He's trying to make himself look serious, but he just looks adorable and sad. "They're not terrible. They just care *a lot*."

So much that he was anxious? He can't seriously believe that's okay.

He must be able to read my thoughts—or I'm sporting the expression he was earlier—because he says, "It's stupid. Forget I said anything. But thanks for helping me out."

"It's not stupid, and don't worry about it. I won't even be mad if you tell them you broke up with me." I muse on that thought for a moment. "You weren't kidding. Cheers to parental issues." I clink my glass against his. "Our parents are shit."

He smiles down at me, and the light reflecting off the disco ball bathes him in a sparkly kaleidoscope of colors. "Cheers to that."

11

SYLAS

Friday, December 13

ONCE WE'RE DONE WITH OUR FIRST PITCHER, IT GETS replaced with another—the liquid green this time.

"'The Grinch,'" the server calls it.

"I have to tell you something." Anna scoots closer to me, and her bare thigh brushes against mine. My breath gets caught when she props her hand on it and her nails dig in like she's trying to steady herself. "Don't judge me, and you can't laugh."

Inhaling sharply, I draw my attention from her hand to her face. Her lips are partially red from the drink, her whiskey eyes are glossed and faintly dazed, and her face is a pretty array of colors thanks to the lights in this place.

My lips lazily rise. "Tell me." I lean in, breathing her in. "I promise I won't judge or laugh."

She draws in closer, fingers curling in and out, faintly scratching my thigh. "I'm a little—no, maybe a *lot* buzzed and I really shouldn't drink any more, but I don't want to stop."

I can't help laughing.

Anna attempts a glare, but she looks too happy for it to have the intended effect. "You said you wouldn't laugh."

My head feels light, face feels warm, and body pulses with bliss, everything around me moving slowly but erratic. "I know. I think I'm buzzed, too."

"There was a lot of tequila in that last one." She licks her lips as if she were trying to taste the drink.

I nod, eyes lasered in on her tongue and how she drags it back and forth. "Too...much."

"But I still want more." She picks up the pitcher and pours green liquid into her cup. "Is that okay with you, or are you ready to go?"

This is when I'm supposed to cut us off and take her home. We've already eaten and I got to spend time with her, but I don't want the night to end.

I slide my glass next to hers. "It's more than okay with me. Plus, they've already brought this over. We shouldn't waste it."

"No, we shouldn't, should we?" She fills my cup, almost spilling some of the liquid as she does. When she sets the pitcher down, she raises her glass and waits for me to do the same.

I do, and ask, "What are we toasting to now?"

She spins in her chair, her crossed legs resting against the inside of my knee. I swallow thickly, thinking of this moment and not the memory of what she felt like when I made her come.

"Everything." She beams.

I'm not sure she notices but she's rubbing her leg against mine. And if she does, she's doing nothing to stop.

"To everything." I'm sure I'm mirroring the same dopey, elated look she's wearing.

We clink our cups against each other and drink. "Vodka." She hums in delight. "This is good."

"Really good." I take a long drink, welcoming the alcohol as it rushes through my veins and numbs the pulsing until I feel like I'm floating. I stretch my arm over the back of her chair. I don't mean to, but my fingers graze her back. "Sorry."

"It's okay." Her eyes descend to my lips briefly before they lift. "I like them there."

"Yeah?" The word sounds rough to my own ears.

"Yeah." Her body softens as I circle the pads of my fingers along her soft skin. "Tell me about yourself."

"What do you want to know?"

I continue gliding my fingers along her shoulder blade, reveling in the way goose bumps break out and she shudders. "I don't know...your accent? Your mom is Brazilian, your dad British. Were you born in the UK?"

I chuckle at the randomness but then sit up, aware she's admitting to knowing about my parents when she claimed not to have a clue. "I thought you didn't know my family?"

"We were hired by them so I kind of did, I just never paid attention. I'm there to do my job. But my roommate, Jenny, did some research. She didn't want me going out with a weirdo." She shudders again and takes a sip of her drink. I make the mistake of looking down when she squeezes her thighs.

Stop touching her, I think, but I can't physically do that.

"I'm glad she didn't think I was a weirdo. I would've hated missing out on seeing you wear this dress."

Her cheeks darken. "Oh no, you're still a weirdo, but I guess you're cool or whatever."

I softly pinch her. "Or whatever?"

"Or whatever," she repeats, voice louder and sultrier. "Come on, tell me about you."

I tell myself to breathe when she rests her free palm on my thigh again. "I was born in New York, but Dad wanted me to be acquainted with his hometown and family in the UK, so I spent a lot of my childhood there. I guess without realizing it, I picked up the accent and it's stuck ever since. It's not as heavy as Dad's, but it's there."

"Mmm..." She hums. "It's hot."

My brows lift, my heart pumping in my ears. "Hot?"

Her blink is slow and expression delayed, as if she's realized what she said. "I could backtrack, but you know what? I won't. I'm sure you hear that a lot, huh?"

I shrug, feigning innocence. A few years ago—I'm embarrassed to admit this—I'd have eaten up the attention. Now it's whatever, but hearing *Anna* say that? I'll speak for the praise alone.

She rolls her eyes but smiles big and dopey. "So, how fluent are you in Spanish?"

"Very. I also speak Portuguese. And I can semi understand and speak French and Italian."

"Wow, little Mr. Overachiever," she muses, her tone playfully patronizing.

"My parents are huge overachievers." I gently pinch her again. "And I'm far from little."

The corner of her lips curve upward into a haughty smirk, then dull into a coy one. "I'm sorry."

My hand freezes on her back. "What are you sorry for?"

"For assuming..."

"Assuming what?" I resume drawing random designs, touching her back everywhere I'm able to.

"That you were going to sacrifice my body or something. Jenny's right, I watch too much TV, but in my defense, rich people do weird things."

My hand halts as I bring my glass to my lips, head tipping back as a laugh bubbles free. I'm not sure what I thought she was going to say, but that wasn't it.

"We usually do that on Tuesdays. You got lucky."

Her lips part. "I got lucky?"

I play into it. "Yeah. Tuesdays are for rituals, followed by the sacrifice. If we wait until the weekend, someone could catch on to it." I take a drink. "As they say, never let them know your next move."

Her lips flatten in what looks like an attempt to smother a laugh, but she's hardly successful. "But today's Friday the thirteenth. Wouldn't today have been the perfect day to complete said ritual?"

I shrug. "It's December. We're feeling the Christmas spirit or whatever."

Anna laughs this time. "Or whatever?"

"Or whatever," I reiterate, keeping my lips in a straight line to look stoic, but she makes it hard.

She takes a long drink. "Well, thanks for not sacrificing me. It wouldn't have been good for my business."

I follow suit, gulping down half of my glass. "You have a business?"

Her face gleams—no, her entire being glows with an exuberant joy. She's inebriated, but I'm positive my buzz has nothing to do with the alcohol and everything to do with being in her presence.

"Yeah, I sell baked goods. Anything and *everything*." She emphasizes that word and now I understand what she meant when she cheersed to *everything*. "Sometimes I take requests, bake things I never have before. I also accommodate all dietary restrictions. I charge half the price, which isn't great for my wallet, but it gives me a chance to get experience. And if my customers are happy, they spread the word."

"Why half?" I prop my elbow on the table, laying my chin on it, absorbing her expressions and the glint in her eyes.

"Because it's easier to convince someone to give me a chance. There're so many bakeries and shops in New York; anyone could simply get their baked goods in those stores. Some are cheaper or just more convenient."

She's not wrong. Everywhere you turn, there's a shop advertising croissants or donuts or whatnot. New York is a competitive city; you either have to step it up or move somewhere else where it's not as busy.

"Consider me persuaded."

Anna's eyes grow wide, and she sits up straight. "What?"

"Bake me something, but charge full price."

"Really? What do you want me to bake? Do you have any

allergies? Any preferences?" She rapidly fires her questions at me. Some of her words are a bit slurred, and giggles trickle out of her mouth freely. "I can bake just about everything."

"Yes, really." I pluck a loose tendril from her bun and twine it around my finger. "I don't have allergies and I'm not picky, so surprise me."

Her eyes bounce left and right in thought, then the brightest smile lifts on her face and she nods. "I know what I'm going to bake for you. When do you want it?"

"Whenever you can make it."

"Okay." She beams, drinks what's left in her glass, and pours more of the drink into it and mine. "I'd make it tonight, but I definitely shouldn't be around an oven. Or a kitchen, for that matter. Also, no scissors. Make sure none are around me."

I chuckle. "That's super specific. Why no scissors?"

"Because I'll end up cutting my hair or trimming my bangs and I'm seriously trying to grow them out."

I brush my fingers across them, careful not to mess them up. "I'm not to be trusted with my credit card when I'm drunk. I'll end up buying stupid shit and have no recollection of it. Or I'll be enticed to do something idiotic, like letting my friends convince me to get a random tattoo."

She sips her drink, eyes drifting to me over the rim. "What did you get and where?"

"Those jellyfish from *SpongeBob*? They're on my pec." I roll my eyes, remembering waking up to my chest feeling sore. I point to where it's located over my shirt.

"You have to show me." She reaches for my hand and swats it away.

"I'll show you..." I lay my hand over hers, flattening it on my chest. "But you'll have to get a tattoo with me."

She incredulously stares at me, brows furrowing. "Like right now?"

"Right now." My heart thrashes at our proximity, beating far faster and harder than before. If she can feel it, she doesn't comment.

"What would we get and where? It's late and—"

"This is New York. Something will be open," I coax.

It's such a rash thing to request, but I'm partially drunk, and being this close to her isn't helping me think clearly.

She squeezes her eyes tight before popping them back open. "Okay, I'll get one with you, but when you get married, you can't tell your wife you got a tattoo with a girl you met at a club and gave an orgasm to. I don't want to be sacrificed in the future. I have so much to live for, and Jenny wouldn't forgive you. She'd hunt you down."

I laugh at her ridiculousness but go along with it anyway. "She'd hunt me down? Wouldn't your husband do that? Wait, I shouldn't assume—do you want to get married?"

My brain is fuzzy, but I remember her telling me she's not interested in relationships.

Dropping my hand, I lean back in my chair and take a drink.

"I do...Not sure when, but I guess I'll know when I know." Her eyes lock with mine. They're a dark forest, enchanting and absorbing. They call to me and I lithely follow. I'm in deep, stuck in a reverie I never want to end.

God, she's beautiful.

I bark a laugh and then she does too. The alcohol has my brain glitching and spazzing out. I don't know what's going on, but I love how I feel and like who I'm next to. I rest my hand on the back of her chair once more, my fingers idly drifting over her exposed skin.

What were we talking about? Tattoos. Right, we're getting tattoos. That's wild. Am I sure I want to do this? I sweep my gaze over her and feel so sure I drain my cup, wanting to quickly finish this pitcher so we can leave.

"What are we going to get?" she says, and I think it over, but nothing comes to mind, although my brain isn't where it should be. It's fixated on how she feels, how beautiful she looks in this dress, how her lips are a mix of green and red from the drink. She keeps licking them and I keep wishing it were me doing that.

"I think I have an idea."

12

ANNA

My head is throbbing.

The incessant pulsing works overtime, spreading down to the tips of my toes.

I groan and pull the blanket over my head. It's abnormally bright in my room, which is strange because it's usually the living room that gets all the sunlight.

The pain in my head makes me forget about the brightness. I snuggle further in my bed but cease all movement when my body connects with another and I hear it groan.

"Stop rubbing your ass against me." Sylas takes a hold of my hip, keeping me in place.

I lie on my side stock-still, still not breathing. *This can't be happening. What did I do? Why is he here? Why does my arm ache? God, my head. What hap—*

My probing questions come to an abrupt halt as I feel something hard poke my butt. *I must've hallucinated that, right?* But my thought gets debunked when I feel it again.

"Shit." He lets go all too fast and shuffles away from me.

I turn, squinting to look at him, hating that my eyesight is unfortunately not the greatest. I'm proud of myself for taking my contacts out last night, but now I wonder where I placed my glasses.

"Here," Sylas says, reaching on top of the sofa then handing me my glasses.

I don't remember leaving them there.

"Thanks." I put them on. His once-blurry figure is now clear.

The blanket pools around his waist, and I notice three things. One, he's shirtless, and his beautiful, sculpted torso is on display. He has thick, corded arms, veins rippling down to the tops of his hands, and abs defined to perfection. Two, we're not in my room; we're on the living room floor. Three, he has a tattoo on his right arm, right below his shoulder. It's new because it has the Saniderm.

Blurry flashbacks of last night filter in my head and then it dawns on me as my arm aches. My gaze drops to it, but it's shielded and I gasp loudly, realizing what I'm wearing. But that's a mistake because my head throbs harder.

"Did we—did we have sex?" I wet my dry lips, faintly tasting a mix of whatever we had to drink last night.

I'm not in my dress. Instead, I'm wearing his white dress shirt, and some of the buttons aren't in the right holes or buttoned at all. I try to piece my memory together, but after we finished the second pitcher, the events are distant and muddled.

"No," he replies, his voice still heavily doused in exhaustion. I shouldn't be focusing on anything but finding out what happened, but the rough, groggy tenor in his voice derails my train of thought.

There's no reason why his voice should sound as attractive as it does.

"No?" I echo.

"No." His eyes roam over me, then the shirt, and stall there a few seconds longer before he meets my stare. He swipes his tongue across his faintly painted red and green lips, and his Adam's apple bobs. "I remember you saying..." He closes his eyes, fingers massaging his temples. "You didn't want to sleep in your dress. So I gave you my shirt because that seemed right."

A fuzzy image of him handing it to me surfaces. I don't know why I didn't grab pajamas when my room is a few feet away, just like my bed is.

"I promise I was on my best behavior." He sounds half amused, half serious.

I believe that. If anything, I'm afraid I'm the one who wasn't. At the bar, I kept placing my hand on his thigh and getting closer to him. I'm certain there were a few times in the night when I wondered why he hadn't made a move.

Now that I think of it, I remember him helping me take my dress off and turning around to give me privacy and me hating that he did.

I made myself desperate last night. I was throwing all the signs, but he didn't reciprocate.

The realization is mortifying. Now I feel sick.

"I would hope so," I quip, hoping I'm masking my humiliation.

I cringe, hating how my brain is playing against me, letting me only remember the moments I'm saying or doing embarrassing things.

Grabbing the blanket, I pull back, adding space between us, but the moment it slips off from around his waist, I see the tent he's sporting in his black dress pants.

My eyes go round, but he doesn't look shy about his erection bulging from his pants. I knew he was large from the night at Salt, but seeing him in this position...fuck.

"Stop looking at it like that. It's your fault." He does nothing but tug at the fabric of his pants a couple of times. I think he's trying to make himself comfortable, but it does nothing but move his dick in a different angle.

I'm flabbergasted. "My fault?"

"You were lying there, rubbing your ass all over me, wearing my shirt."

"You act like I did it on purpose. I didn't know you were behind me."

A crease forms between his eyebrows, his jaw clenches. "Who did you think was behind you?"

"No one." I thump his leg. "I thought I was alone in my bed. I thought we parted ways after the second pitcher…" My thoughts scatter, the rest of my words getting lost as I'm hit with something.

Tattoos.

"We got tattoos." My mouth gapes open at his nod. "Oh my gosh," I squeak, and he drops his head back and bursts into laughter. It's deep and rumbly. I get lost in the rapt sound and find myself laughing too.

"I swear it was a mutual decision." His laughter subsides. "But we were also pretty wasted. I'm certain we got more drinks after getting them…I think. No…we definitely did." He pauses, pondering a thought. "If it makes you feel any better, I let you pick and swore to you I wouldn't tell my wife we got matching tattoos."

"We got *matching* tattoos?" I balk, staring at him and his fresh tattoo in astonishment.

My hand immediately reaches for my arm where it's sore, but I don't press my palm against it. Instead, I undo the button, not caring that I'm exposing my chest to him. Either way, he's already seen one of my breasts, and I'm wearing silicone nipple covers.

I shrug the sleeve down, exposing my left arm, and gasp at the ink etched on my skin.

"You're not upset, are you?" He drags his fingers through his disheveled hair. "Shit, I—"

I blink, snapping out of it. "No, I'm not upset." I chuckle, still in disbelief. "I'm just…I got…" I scoff a laugh, bewildered. It's really pretty. A small chain holds a disco ball, then what looks like a string hangs from the bottom of it holding an upside-down whisk. At the tip of the wires, there's another string holding a single hockey skate. And around them, tiny stars are scattered. "A hockey skate. A *hockey* skate, Sylas. I know nothing about hockey. I've never even been to a game."

He appears relieved, but then his head rears back and his eyes narrow. He looks...offended? "You've never been to a game?"

I shrug. "Never thought about it until I moved here. Even then I didn't care for it."

We're a Division 1 school. All the sports here are a big deal but KYU is most known for hockey. Still, sports never called my attention, and I've never had time for them.

He stares at me, at once insulted and disappointed. "That's going to have to change. You're coming to a game and—"

I smile at the excitement that exudes him. "I can't, I work. I really can't afford to take any days off."

"Right." He deflates.

I hate that he looks genuinely upset. I could take one day off. I never have, but now that I have a little extra from what he gave me, it wouldn't hurt. No, what am I thinking? I seriously can't be considering taking a day off for a guy I hardly know. What's wrong with me?

His money won't ever run out, but mine will if I'm not smart about it.

"Morning," Jenny singsongs, padding out of her room in a fluffy pink robe. "Oh fuck." She stops in her tracks, eyes widening and eyebrows rocketing to her hairline. She glances from my open shirt to where Sylas is on the floor, still sporting a tent in his pants. He's not as hard as before, but he's so big it doesn't even matter. *Jesus.*

He snatches the blanket, laying it over his legs to cover himself up.

"Morning," he supplies, sounding more awake than he did a few seconds ago.

"It's not what it looks like," I blurt just as she's about to spin around. I stand, my head spinning a little before it steadies. "We got matching tattoos."

"No way." Her eyes shift from his arm to mine. "Holy fuck."

She's in front of me in a flash, grabbing my arm gingerly and inspecting the art. "And they're matching? You guys are insane... wait, you didn't elope last night, did you?"

Sylas and I look at each other. We don't say it out loud, but we're thinking it. *No, that couldn't have happened. It definitely didn't happen.*

"No..." He's the first to speak up. "We just got these and were kind of drunk."

"Kind of?" She makes a *pfft* sound. "You guys were drunk as shit, all over the place, and loud as fuck, but I appreciate neither of you throwing up or breaking anything."

Sylas grins. "Sorry about that. I had no intention of staying, but *someone* just couldn't let go of me."

"You're not saying I asked you to stay?"

He nods and so does Jenny.

"You basically begged him," she says under her breath.

I frown, feeling more than embarrassed now. *So I threw myself at him, got matching tattoos, and begged him to stay. Great.*

I shrug it off, pretending I'm not upset and annoyed at myself. While he's nice, I can't pretend that after today or even after the break, we'll become friends and hang out.

Plastering on a smile, I look at him. "I'm going to brush my teeth and change to give you your shirt back." I don't wait for him to say something. I slip out of the living room, Jenny on my heels.

"You okay?" she asks as we step into my room.

"Yes—no." I undo the rest of the buttons, remove the shirt, and change into something else. "I'm embarrassed. Find me in the dictionary next to *desperate*," I grumble. "You should've kicked him out and slapped some sense into me."

Her lips twitch. "Stop being dramatic. He wasn't rushing to leave. Matter of fact, I'm certain he wanted to stay. Once you gave him the green light, he was quick to make himself comfortable, helping you out of your dress and giving you his shirt. It was honestly really sweet."

"So you saw all of this happening and didn't do anything?" I glare at her.

She laughs. "Don't look at me like that. You wanted *him* to help you, but I did watch from a distance, making sure he didn't do something stupid, and he didn't. I also tried to get you both to your bed, but once you hit that floor, it was game over. I didn't have it in me to fight with you, and I knew he wasn't going to budge. Whatever you said, he did."

"Really?" There's a tiny flutter in my stomach, but I force it to stop as I step into our bathroom to brush my teeth. "Still screams desperate."

"Not desperate when he happily did as you said." She smirks, lifting a shoulder in a half shrug.

I stare at my reflection, face pinched in a grimace. My makeup is smudged under my eyes, my hair is barely hanging on to the bun I put it in last night, and bobby pins stick out.

But how I look flies out of my mind as I stare at the tattoo. I still can't believe I got it and that it matches his.

Blinking last night away, I finish making myself presentable. Then I look for the extra toothbrushes I know we have and head back to the living room.

Jenny goes to her room, but not before winking at me and wagging her eyebrows suggestively, which I ignore.

Sylas is looking down at the table where my journal is at. "Hey! You know that's an invasion of privacy."

He jolts, standing up straighter. I should've thought it through because he stands in all of his six-foot-four glory, shirtless, abs rippling, and despite the tired look on his face, the ruggedness makes him even more attractive.

"I wasn't trying to snoop. It was left open, and you wrote in bright red. It was hard not to look. Sorry."

I'm weak because he's smiling apologetically, dimples indented on each cheek, and the sunlight is shining on him like a halo. I'm struggling to remember what I was saying.

My journal, right.

"I swear I didn't look through it. Just the page it was on."

"It's fine." I hand him the shirt and the extra toothbrush. "It's not a diary, just a journal I fill with random stuff and my recipes."

He takes the shirt and toothbrush but doesn't pull his hand away. "Random stuff?" he balks. "Did you really draw that?"

"Yeah." I feel stupidly shy at the awed look on his face. "It's not my best work."

"Not your best work? That drawing looks so realistic." He towers over me, and his smile is luminous. "And it made me hungry."

I chuckle, brushing my bangs away. "Thanks." Compliments and praise sometimes make me awkward. Accepting them feels strange, especially when it's nothing that should be talked about. Why am I overthinking what he said? I distance myself from him. "Anyway, the bathroom is over there."

His eyebrows scrunch and he looks like he wants to say something, but then he disappears down the hall. When he returns, he's got his shirt on and it's buttoned up, and his hair is damp and finger-combed back.

"You smell really good."

"What?" I ask, bemused.

"I mean, my shirt. It—whatever you had on last night smells really good. My walk of shame won't be so bad now."

I roll my eyes, grinning. "You leaving is *not* a walk of shame."

"Kind of feels like it..." The tease in his voice makes me feel jittery inside.

We stall in the middle of the living room, unable to look away or speak either. I want to say something, like maybe ask if he wants to stay, but I did enough begging last night. He may have been nice, but it's still embarrassing.

"I guess I should go."

"Yeah..." *Stay* clings to the tip of my tongue, but I don't expel it.

He walks to the front door and slips on his shoes. "Thanks again for coming to the auction and going along with the fake dating bit, and everything else." He peeks at his covered arm then at mine. "I promise not to tell my wife."

I give him a warning stare, pointing my finger at him. "You better not. Jenny will hunt you down. Remember that."

He grins. "I'll never forget." It sounds like there's another meaning behind those words, but I don't dwell on it. "Bye, Anna."

"Bye, Sylas." I smile at him one last time before he walks out, closing the door behind him.

13

SYLAS

Saturday, December 14

"You look like shit" is how Thea greets me when I slump down on the chair in front of her.

My sister and I stay busy, so we hardly have time for each other these days. Once a month, we make an effort to grab a meal and catch up, which is exactly what we've come to do at In A Jam.

I shove my sunglasses up the bridge of my nose and give her an indolent wave. "Morning."

"Morning?" I hear the amusement in her voice, but I avoid eye contact. "It's three in the afternoon. Did you just wake up?"

Slouching back on my chair, I pick up my menu and browse through the items.

After I left Anna's, I went home, showered, and laid in bed, hoping I'd fall asleep, but every few minutes, flashbacks of last night emerged. Every time I attempted to shut the memories down, another would pop up.

Instead of fighting against them or trying to sleep, I let myself get immersed in what I could remember.

After getting a proper look at my new tattoo and giving it a clean, I looked her up on Instagram then spent an ungodly amount of time staring at every picture. It's lame, really, but I couldn't stop clicking. I also looked through her baking account.

She wasn't kidding when she said she bakes everything. There were different types of dessert, and they all looked so damn pretty and delicious.

Along with those two accounts, I found out she has a VSCO. I know Thea has one, but I'd never been enticed to download it until just a few hours ago. And doing so led me to spend a few more hours skimming through each picture she's ever uploaded. They all look like they're behind the scenes, the ones that didn't make the cut on Instagram. Regardless, they're just as pretty.

Because I spent a pathetic amount of time stalking her, I had to push Thea's and my reservation.

"Yeah, I just woke up." I fake a yawn.

She grows quiet, forcing me to look up at her. She's wearing this creepy Cheshire-like grin on her face. "Does this have something to do with the hottie with the body in the green dress? The girl you told Mom and Dad is *your girlfriend*?" She hikes a brow, inquisitive eyes boring into me. Thea was at the auction, so I know she witnessed Anna bidding on me. "The girl you asked out, according to Marc."

Dammit, Marcello.

"She's not my girlfriend. Mom and Dad haven't shut up about Florence and me since we were in the womb. You know I'm over their bullshit; I had to say something."

"Yeah, I figured as much. But that aside, did you really ask her out on a date? Like an *actual* date where no sex was involved?"

"We're not going to talk about it."

"But—"

"We said we'd never talk about our sex lives. So, let's not talk about it."

"That was before I found out you were going to hang out with a girl in a way that didn't involve clothes coming off," she retorts and leans forward, her face dimming into a supportive, soft expression—or as tender as she can make it. Because she's far from soft and tender. "Who is she?"

Thea and I usually don't talk about these kinds of things because what person wants to hear about who their sibling is fucking? I don't ask her, and she doesn't ask me. Though I know she's heard about me on campus, which isn't my fault because people love to talk.

"How do you know clothes didn't come off?" I arch a brow.

"I don't, but you don't look like you had one of *those* nights."

"What kind of night do you think I had?"

"I don't know, you tell me." She pauses, taking a sip of her water. "Marc said you looked a little jealous about Alex wanting to ask her out," she says, a lofty grin curling her lips. "Were you? Does someone have a crush?"

Fucking Marc. They just *had* to be best friends, didn't they.

I roll my eyes. "It's—it's not..." I stumble and hesitate. What's wrong with me? "It's not like that. I didn't have sex with her last night because...because I don't need to have sex with every girl I hang out with. I'm done talking about this. Plus, we were drunk."

There is no way in hell I'd do anything with Anna in that state.

She snickers. "You have a crush. How fucking cute."

My heart does that weird manic thing where it beats out of control to the point it feels like it's going to explode. My hands sweat at the thought, and a flashback of me holding her hand when she was about to get her tattoo surfaces.

"I have to tell you a secret," Anna whispers, but she doesn't do a good job because the tattoo artist, Anya, side-eyes her before focusing back on getting everything ready.

"Yeah, tell me."

"I'm a little nervous. Can you hold my hand?"

"Of course." I immediately take it in mine, intertwining our fingers. "Why don't you keep your eyes on me?"

She nods, then says, "I'm really glad I'm doing this with you."

My lips feel heavy as they lift higher, my face warm and body tingly. "Me too. I'm happy it's you."

"It's not a crush," I deadpan.

"Sure," Thea drawls mockingly, her expression morphing into a thoughtful, tentative one. "Mom and Dad are angry about your fake girlfriend."

"They'll be okay."

"I don't think they will be." She drags her finger along the rim of her glass. "You should've seen them, Sy. Mom was speaking in Portuguese, and Dad had that look on his face."

"It'll be fine. They'll get over it." I don't know how much I believe that, but she's my fake girlfriend; it's not like I'm getting married to her. Soon, I'll tell them we broke up and that'll be the end of it. Or they'll act like we're not together and never bring it up. "Anyway, do you think Dad will disown me if I bail on the Christmas party?"

I don't care for big celebrations. I don't even care for my birthday, but if there's one holiday I hate, it's Christmas.

Every year, Mom and Dad throw the most over-the-top party on Christmas Eve. They invite all our family members and their friends and make a show of what a happy family we are. Thea and I have no other choice but to play into it, smiling as our parents boast about us as if they don't spend every minute of the day behind closed doors criticizing everything we do.

"Kiss your trust fund goodbye. Matter of fact, expect all your accounts to be frozen. I bet they'll even block your access to the penthouse," she answers cheerfully, but behind the levity, the seriousness is loud and clear.

I sigh. "I'll be there."

"Look on the bright side, I'll be there and now that they think you have a girlfriend, they'll leave you alone and Florence will fuck off."

"God, I hope so." I remove my sunglasses and rub my tired eyes. The action makes me think of Anna and how she told me she couldn't sleep with her contacts on. Then she had me look for her glasses and I laid them on the sofa so I could grab them easily when she woke up.

"You and this girl—"

"Her name is Anna, and there is no us. Move on."

She peers up at me from her lashes, a supercilious smirk on her face. "But have you?"

"Have I what?" I ask, skimming the menu.

"Moved on?"

"What is there to move on from? We just hung out. Friends do that all the time. The same way you and Marc do, unless there's something I need to know about?"

Her face scrunches. "Gross, no. I'm just saying. You seem off."

"I'm tired. It was a long night. Drop it." The pulse in my temple throbs painfully. "What are you getting?"

She's staring at me, but I don't look at her. I don't know what she expects to hear, but there's nothing to say. While last night was one of the best nights I've ever had, it was nothing more than two people hanging out.

We don't have practice today but after lunch earlier, I had to get on the ice. I needed to think of anything but Thea's words.

I don't have a crush. I'm not sure exactly what a crush would entail, but I definitely don't have one.

I hear a whipping sound but I'm too late to move because I feel it smack my back. "What the hell are you thinking about? I've never seen you this distracted. Focus," Marc warns, removing his glove and helmet to wipe the sweat off his forehead.

"I'm focused."

I asked Marc to meet me at the arena. We've been here for almost two hours, working on drills and stickhandling. We're not pushing too hard, seeing as I'm still hungover.

We finish off the final thirty minutes with 1v1. Him on defense, me on offense. Even though my head pounds, I manage to score on him.

As we skate over to where our waters are, I'm praying the conversation doesn't stray to the elephant in the room. But it's stupid of me to think he won't ask. This is my best friend; he doesn't give a fuck.

"Was your date so bad last night it's making you play like shit?" I aim my bottle in his direction, squeezing it, but he manages to skate back before the water lands on him. "I'll take that as a yes."

"No, this has nothing to do with my date. I told you I'm hungover. And if I played like shit, why did I score on you?"

He snorts. "Hungover? You're full of shit. I've seen you play hungover. This has nothing to do with that."

It was only one time, but I made sure to work hard so Coach wouldn't bust my ass. He still caught on and I got punished for it.

"Also, what the fuck?" I give another squeeze of my bottle. "Why'd you tell Thea about Anna?"

He shrugs, dodging the stream of water. "She asked, and you know I tell her everything. She was going to find out regardless. You told your *parents* Anna is your girlfriend, you dumb fuck."

"You know when you said you'd be my best friend, I didn't think you'd make her your best friend, too." I glare at him. "God, do you two really talk about everything?"

"Everything." He blows me a kiss. "Don't overdo your jealousy. You already did enough of that yesterday."

"I wasn't jealous. I was annoyed that Alex continued to ask when I'd told him to fuck off." And he still had the audacity to follow her on Instagram. I don't think now's the time to mention that because he'll think I'm jealous, which I'm not.

"Thea was right, you're crushing so hard." He laughs and skates away when I throw my bottle at his head. It misses him completely, plopping hard against the ice.

"I'm not." I skate after him with my stick, but he swerves left and right, laughing maniacally.

"Sylas has a crush! Sylas has a crush!" he shouts, his voice and the sound of skates slicing against the ice reverberating around the empty arena.

I stop chasing after him, not sure why I even began. Now he's really going to assume I like her. "You're a childish fuck."

"And you're a stupid fuck." He skates idly up next to me, picking up my bottle and tossing it over. "So what if you like her? What's wrong with that?"

I think about it hard and really let it settle. *What* is *wrong with that?*

"We hardly know each other. I met her about eight days ago. We're too busy to make it work." I remove my helmet, running my fingers through my sweat-drenched hair. "I don't know if she likes me like that. How do I even know if I *like* like her?"

"*Dio.*" He pinches the bridge of his nose, shaking his head. Then he fixes me with a look that screams *You're fucking stupid.* "Get to know her. Time is just an illusion. Make space in your calendar. And yes, you dumb fuck, you have a crush. Who gets matching tattoos with a girl they hardly know?"

"We were drunk," I counter pathetically.

He saw it in the locker room and asked about it. I should've kept my mouth shut.

"Regardless, you have a crush. Own it."

"How can I own it when I'm not even sure I really do? We're not going to stand here and act like Anna isn't hot because we both know she is. What if this is just me lusting because she's attractive?" I'm not trying to sound like an ass, I'm genuinely curious.

I've never been in a relationship. I have nothing against them, but it's never been something I want. But...I don't know...I kind of like the idea of spending more time with Anna. We don't need to be undressed for it to happen. We could talk about anything and everything and I'd be okay with that. We wouldn't even need to talk, we could just watch a movie and maybe cuddle. Jesus, since when do I like to do that?

He hums and scratches the back of his head. "I don't know. Why don't you find out?"

"How?" I pause, picking up my phone as it vibrates with a text.

> Dad: If Anna isn't working, let's have dinner tomorrow.

> Dad: I'd like to get to know your girlfriend.

"Why do you look like you're about to pass out?"

I show him my phone.

"Let me guess, he's not asking." I nod and he rolls his eyes. "Sounds like my dad."

Our dads go way back and have a lot in common. They love money and the ability to tell people what to do.

He looks pensive for a moment until his entire demeanor brightens. "Take her. Play up the whole charade, get to know her, and if you fall for her then you fall. If you don't then at least you gave it a shot and then you can fake break up."

"She works a lot, and she didn't agree to keep this up." I can't imagine Anna wanting to keep pretending to date me or spend time with my parents.

He shrugs. "It's either you do it or your dad knows you lied. You know he won't stop until you comply."

I hate how right he is.

"And the solution to her work issue is to pay her," he suggests simply. "Tell her to take some days off until you figure this out. Bam! Your problem is solved. You're welcome."

"You act like it's that easy." Though it does sound like it is, but would Anna agree?

"I'm just saying, she must need the money. It can't hurt to ask. Stop being a little bitch and ask her."

I flip him off as I consider it.

14

ANNA

My wet hair is dripping onto the floor, creating tiny puddles every time I pause to gather my panicked thoughts.

I had no time to dry it or put it in a towel because Jenny had blown up my phone with egregious news.

"You still there?" Her voice crashes through the chaotic shouting in my head.

I pace our apartment from the entrance through the living room and kitchen and down to our bedrooms and back up. Every so often, I struggle to breathe and not lose my shit again and have to stop. "Yeah, here. I'm...thinking."

We just got an email from our landlord, Jerry, stating he's raising our rent again but this time by five hundred dollars. He wants to renovate the building to make sure the tenants get the best living experience, among other things. It's a load of bullshit. They gave that exact reason last year, just worded differently.

Jenny went to see her grandma again, so she's not here to freak out with me.

I know I have the money Sylas gave me, but after giving half to Jenny as promised, I planned to save the rest for culinary school and bills.

"I don't know how we're going to manage," she breathes out. We're barely hanging on as it is. "We could…" Her voice wavers and she murmurs something under her breath. "We could…This is bullshit," she grumbles, then goes silent. I drag my phone away from my ear to make sure she didn't hang up. "I have an idea."

The hesitation in her voice has me on edge. "Yeah?"

"We could move in with my grandma."

"You moved out for a reason," I remind her.

Jenny's grandma lives with other family members who know no bounds of personal space. They hardly have space as it is; I don't want to be the reason they have less of it. She also lives an hour from here, so commuting would be a nightmare.

"I know." She sighs. "That's the last place I want to go back to, but it's the only option that comes to mind."

My socked feet squelch with every step I take, the puddles larger than I had realized.

I compile a list of apartments we've looked through before, but I know they'll either cost as much as we pay now or more. They'll also be smaller, but that's the least of our worries. I don't know if they'll even be available this time of year.

"I don't know what we'll do." Dread pierces her words.

"I—I," I stammer, tipping my head back and staring at the brown water stains on the ceiling. Tears prick my eyes and my nose burns, but I refuse to let myself cry. If I do, I'll do the stupid thing and call my parents, and that's the last thing I want to do. My head throbs as I try to think of something, but nothing comes to mind. Except for not wanting to stress out Jenny more than she already is. "Let me think it through. You just worry about your grand—"

"No, I can drive back and—"

"No," I insist. "Stay with your grandma. She needs you and I know you want to be with her. Let me think it through, and once I come up with something, I'll call you. Okay?"

Jenny is the most selfless person I've ever met. She has gone above and beyond for me, and I want to do the same for her.

She goes silent again, but I know she hasn't hung up. She's thinking it through and at her groan, I know she's going to concede. "Okay, but I'll be thinking too. We're going to be okay."

"We are. We'll be okay." I force a smile despite her not being here to see it. "Say hi to her for me."

I hang up, stop at the kitchen, and drop my head on the laminate countertop.

I have no clue what I'm going to do. I'm not tutoring anyone because we're on winter break. I make good tips at the restaurant but not enough to cover a rent hike. Cleaning is going okay, but I'm not doing it as much because of the break. My business is doing okay, but I'm not making hundreds.

It's the holidays, so surely someone will hire me. They have to. I'll drop to my knees and beg. That's how desperate I am.

"Fuck you, Jerry!"

Just as I push off the counter, my phone vibrates in my hand. When I look at the screen, I'm stunned.

Sylas: I need a favor

I have no idea what he could want from me, but that doesn't stop my heart from racing or the stupid flutters in my stomach from erupting. My gaze dips to the tattoo on my arm, my regret now tenfold.

My fingers twitch to reply, but I stop myself. Would I look desperate if I answered him right away? I shouldn't, but curiosity gets the better of me.

Me: Not sure if I should be offended you didn't greet me or happy you're getting straight to the point

Sylas: You want me to greet you?

Me: Obviously! Where are your manners?

Sylas: Left them somewhere in the corner of
Salt where I made you come

My jaw drops, and a disbelieving laugh slips past my mouth. We haven't talked about it much, and I figured we'd continued to ignore it.

A towel is the only thing wrapped around my body, but it feels like I'm wearing thick layers because I'm burning up thinking of that night.

Sylas: I could make it happen again. Just say
the word

Do I want it to happen again? Do I want that? Should I say something? *No. Stop being horny. You have bigger issues than thinking about orgasms.*

Me: What's the favor?

Sylas: Hi, Anna. How are you doing?

My lips stretch in a way that makes me anxious. Why am I smiling?

Me: Hi, Sylas. I'm okay. How are you?

Sylas: Better now that you've answered

It's so corny but I'm smiling so big, my cheeks ache.

Me: 😳 Stop

Sylas: Stop what?

Me: Whatever it is you're doing

Sylas: What am I doing?

Me: You know exactly what

Sylas: I don't. Tell me

Me: You're trying to be cute or whatever because you need a favor

Sylas: Or whatever

Me: Please don't send me that emoji. Are you going to tell me or what?

Sylas: Come meet me

That kills everything inside me. It's eleven p.m. The last thing I want to do is go out. It's brutally cold outside.

Me: NO! I just got out of work and I'm exhausted. Tell me now or I'm blocking you

Sylas: Come meet me. I promise it'll be worth it

Me: Nothing is worth going out at this time of day. Especially to see you

Sylas: You're breaking my heart, meu bem

Me: That sounds like a personal problem. I'd have to have it to do that. And what does that mean?

Sylas: Now you have it. It means my dear

Oh God, my heart. Stay still, calm down, I tell it.

Me: You're so lame. Please don't tell me this is how you flirt?

Sylas: I'm not flirting

Me: Then what do you call this lame attempt
at whatever it is you're doing?

Sylas: My attempt at getting you to smile. Did
it work?

My lips could be touching my ears from how big I'm smiling.
I'm fucked.

Me: No. I'm not easily impressed

Sylas: But easily convinced. Easily…

Me: Easily what?

Sylas: Oops. Meant to say easy* At least you
were that night, right? Be easy for me. Come
meet me. Please, meu bem

I should block him, but instead my body has the audacity to
easily react to that. My core tightens as do my nipples and a throb
grows between my thighs.

Me: No. You come to me

Sylas: I can do that

My fingers hover above the keyboard.

Me: You can? You'll come?

Sylas: I'm here. Open the door

My gaze jumps to the front door then down to the towel
wrapped around my body and the trail of puddles I left.

Me: Have you been here this entire time?

Sylas: A few minutes now. You really think I'd
make you come to me? What kind of asshole
do you think I am?

I'm stuck in a stupor. I don't immediately reply until a few knocks on my door echo around my apartment. "Hi, Anna," I hear on the other side.

My pulse quickens, but my body freezes in place. I glance down at the towel then the puddles again.

> Me: The kind of asshole that doesn't warn me

I grab a wad of paper towels and clean up the mess I made. Then I run to my room, throw something on, and wrap my hair in a towel.

When I pick up my phone again, there's three messages from him.

> Sylas: I wanted to surprise you. Surprise!!

> Sylas: I'll leave if you don't want me here

> Sylas: I should've warned you, but that defeats the purpose of a surprise

> Me: You must be desperate for this favor

My reply is nonchalant, but I feel everything but that. It's embarrassing and probably pathetic, but I'm happy that he's here. I shouldn't be, but I am. I tell myself to chill out as I open the door.

He stands on the other side wearing a beanie, a thick black jacket, and light gray joggers. The tip of his nose is faintly pink as are the apples of his cheeks. When his eyes land on me, his dimples appear and his eyes brighten.

"Very...desperate." His gaze sweeps over me in a long, slow motion. I'm not wearing anything cute, just an oversized graphic T-shirt and sweatpants. "Were you surprised?"

I keep my face blasé but my lips twitch, tempted to rise. "You showed up unexpectedly. How else am I supposed to react?"

"Ecstatically. Jumping for joy," he delivers wryly. "It's me we're talking about."

I don't mean to, but I laugh, and that makes him chuckle. "You think too much of yourself."

"I do." He shrugs indifferently like he doesn't care about how that'll come off. It should be annoying, but I find it hot.

Stepping to the side, I welcome him in and exhale quietly as I stand behind him, getting myself together.

"What's so important you decided to show up now? You know, it's close to midnight." I motion for him to sit on the other end of the sofa.

It's weird having him here. He's so tall, taking up so much space I struggle to breathe. Just a few weeks ago we knew nothing of each other; now we're talking as if we've been friends for a while and getting matching tattoos. But as odd as this is, it's strange how comfortable I feel around him.

"I do. That's why I'm here. It's important." He shifts so he's facing me.

We're sitting on opposite ends of the sofa, but we could be sitting miles away from each other and it still wouldn't feel far enough. He feels so close, chills run down my body and it tenses with anticipation.

"Okay, I'm all ears."

"I need you to be my girlfriend again."

I laugh because there's no way that came out of his mouth. "No, seriously, what's the favor?"

He stares stoically. "No, seriously, I need you to be my girl-friend *again*."

My mouth splits open, but I'm too stunned to speak. A part of me wants to believe he's messing with me, but the grave expression on his face tells me he's being serious.

"What? Why?"

He exhales a fatigued breath, fishes out his phone from his pocket, and shows me the screen. "Because of this."

Dad: If Anna isn't working, let's have dinner tomorrow.

Dad: I'd like to get to know your girlfriend.

"Oh." I finish reading the message and he drops his phone in his lap, puffing a frustrated breath.

What did I think was going to happen? Really should've seen this coming.

"Yeah..." He's staring straight ahead like he's contemplating his life's purpose. "So, what do you say?"

I scratch the back of my head, feeling utterly perplexed. "I get they want to keep it in the circle, but why don't you just tell your parents you don't want to marry Flor—"

"I can't. There's a lot at stake. Too much I'll lose," he explains vaguely.

For a long moment, I say nothing. I get where he's coming from—kind of. My parents, at least Mom, liked to control every aspect of my life until I decided to shut that down, but doing that caused me to lose them and their help. I can't begin to imagine what's at stake for him.

Still, I don't have the time to play pretend. I'm past the *we don't know each other* hiccup because we got matching tattoos and have opened up to each other. Despite that, I have to work and have my own things to figure out.

"I'm sorry but I have to work and—"

"I'll pay you."

"For fake dating you?" He nods. "No! That's weird."

"I'm going to sound like an ass, but weren't you just freaking out about your rent?"

I'm taken aback. "How long were you outside?"

He stretches his long arm along the back of the sofa. "Long enough to know you need money."

I stand, irritation clouding my thoughts. "No. I'm not going to be your fake girlfriend for a few dollars."

He rises to his feet, removing his beanie to drag his fingers through his hair. "You didn't even ask how much I'm going to give you. And just so you know, it'll be enough so you won't need to work next semester."

"Get out of here." I may be overreacting, but this has got to be some kind of prank. I step back, feeling nothing but annoyed.

"Why are you mad?" He wrinkles his brow, face twisted in bewilderment.

"Why am I mad?" I scoff. "You can't be serious."

He nods like that should be obvious.

"Is this another thing rich people do when they're bored?" From the way he acted the night of the auction, I understood I needed to play along. His dad was intense. But this can't be real. Enough I wouldn't need to work? Yeah fucking right.

"I'm serious, Anna. You really think I'd come all the way over here just to fuck with you? Yes, *we rich people do weird shit*," he sardonically remarks. "But we also don't like to waste our time. I really need your help and, yes, I'm going to compensate you, although it'll probably never feel enough considering you have to put up with my parents."

I fold my arms against my chest. I don't know why, but I know he's not messing with me. Still, this feels so bizarre. "And what happens when they want to see me again? How long do we need to keep this up for?"

His lips quirk up. "You keep playing along until the end of next semester."

"So, I'm supposed to drop everything for you?"

"No. Not *everything*."

My teeth clench. "This isn't funny."

"Never said it was," he reasons. "I'm paying you—shouldn't that be enough?"

"God. Everything is so easy for you people, huh?" Maybe I'm being irrational, but what if he decides he doesn't need me? Or what if he falls in love with Florence and all of this is for nothing? There are many more things I could list, but I'd give myself a headache over it.

"Some things are." He shrugs unapologetically. "I get all of this is hard to believe and maybe I'm coming off as an asshole. I'm sorry. I didn't mean to spring this on you, but I'm going to pay you. And don't act like it's wrong that I am because it's not. It's money for fake dating, not for sex." He's not smiling, but there is a mischievous twinkle in his eyes. "Unless…"

That makes me feel hot…makes me feel… "What do I look like? What's *wrong* with you?"

He places his beanie back on his head. "That's why I didn't include it in the proposal."

I swallow hard. "So you thought about it?"

Sylas stares at me for a beat. "Can you help me?"

"Answer me," I demand.

His jaw tics. "So you can slap me? Nah."

"I told you I don't solve my problems throwing hands."

It's really stupid that I want to know. But now my head is in the gutter and I'm thinking about the night at Salt and he's here and we're alone.

What is wrong with me? I shouldn't want to know. I'm about to tell him to forget it, but then he answers.

"I did. I know it sounds wrong. I know it's demeaning, but I'm not going to pretend like I haven't thought about that night. You liked what I said and did. You got off on that, and I did too." He wets his lips, chest expanding. "But I didn't suggest it because I know how wrong it sounds."

I drop down on the sofa, resting my elbows on my thighs, chin on my fists. He crouches in front of me, his hands on my knees. Despite the position, he still feels imposing.

"Anna—"

"I don't see this working out." I meet his eyes.

"How would you know if we haven't given it a chance?" There's a playfulness in his voice that makes me smile a little. "I'll be the best pretend boyfriend ever."

"We've never been in relationships. There's no way they believe we *like* each other."

"We faked it just fine the other night." He grins. "And, well, Salt wasn't fake for me. So…"

"Because it was an in-the-moment kind of thing. I wasn't thinking. I was—"

"Doing what felt right in the moment." His eyes are full of heat and hunger, a reminder of both nights. "I did the same and I think we can make it work. We're good together."

I'm stuck. I don't know what to make of this. "I don't know. I have a lot going on. I can't drop what I'm doing to be there every time you need me."

"You don't have to drop everything because I probably won't need much from you. It's dinner for now and then we'll take it as it comes." I swallow as he absently rubs his thumbs along my knees. "And I'm going to be upfront because, fuck it, if you want another night like Salt, if you want—no *need* a distraction from the chaos of the world and our parents, I can do that, too. I can be your distraction, and you can be mine. No one has to know what we do except for us. And I'm all for going exclusive too."

I sit up, eyes widening and mouth going dry. I didn't expect him to be so direct, but it shouldn't have been a surprise. The few days I've known him, he's never seemed shy about what he wants.

"Think about it. Why play the back-and-forth game when we both know what we want, what we like, how we like it. If you don't want to do it for me, do it for you. You need the money. Let me give it to you, and in return, you give me your time and body," he presses, not appearing the least bit embarrassed.

"I hate how easily you say this." *And how, disturbingly, I also love it.*

He smirks, and his usual pale green eyes are now a pair of dark, sharp emeralds. "I know, but hating it won't change anything. Think about it."

"You really think I'm going to let you use my body for money? You think I'm that desperate?" I wish I were mad, but I'm strangely turned on.

"It's just you and me." He pulls back a little. "I'm honest with you, so be honest with me. Tell me you're not thinking about it. Tell me you don't want me to have you however I want. Tell me, Anna," he goads.

"I've never done this. I don't know if I'll like it again."

His jaw hardens and his hooded eyes incinerate me from the inside out. "Do you want to find out?"

My thighs squeeze at the pressure that grows between them. I shouldn't do this, but I desperately want to find out. "I do."

15

SYLAS

SHE LOOKS CURIOUS, EXCITED, AND MORE THAN A little intimidated. Her whiskey eyes are dark and dilated, and her breaths are rapid, making her chest rise fast and drop even faster. Her face down to her neck is flushed in a rosy glow.

I genuinely didn't come with the intention of doing this. But once I saw her, breathed her in, I couldn't resist. Even so, I wouldn't have gone through with using her body for money. I was going to immediately shut it down, backtrack, or make it about the favor, but then I saw it. Her eyes glossed over, I heard her swallow, caught on to the way she subtly attempted to clench her thick thighs.

Any rational thought I had about not demeaning her flew out of my head.

"We need a safe word." I cup her neck.

"Safe word? Why? How intense is this going to get?" She wets her lips.

I follow her tongue. "It's not. I've never done this either, so it might end up being a strong dose of vanilla." My lips lift at the tint of amusement that flashes on her face. "But it's good to be cautious. The last thing I want is to do something you're uncomfortable with."

She cocks a brow. "You've never degraded someone? You seemed like you knew what you were doing at the club."

"It felt right with you. Watching and feeling your body and how it reacts to me. The same way I'm doing now."

"You're doing it now?" She goes taut in my hand as I brush my thumb over her jawline, to the center of her chin, dragging it down the column of her neck. I repeat the motion, reveling in how she writhes.

"You react every time my thumb reaches your chin." I slip my hand around her throat, squeezing it, but not too hard. "You're so easy, Anna, and I haven't even done anything."

"You're the one who's hard," she retorts, cupping my erection through my sweats. "If anyone is easy, it's you."

I grind my teeth, fighting a groan as she strokes me. "Being hard doesn't mean shit. I wake up like this most mornings. But you, on the other hand—I know you have to work for it. I know you have to be physically and mentally stimulated to get wet. And right now, you are. I bet if I slipped my fingers inside your panties, you'd be dripping. Because you're nothing but an easy whore who'll do anything for money. Isn't that right?"

Her mouth pops open, a deep divot forming between her eyebrows. But she doesn't pull away, doesn't kick me out. She stays planted where she stands, releasing her hand from around me.

My cock throbs at how much I liked calling her that and how she does nothing but take it.

"Isn't that right?" I repeat, squeezing her throat again.

She nods, her olive skin tone now a pretty shade of crimson.

"No, say it." I squeeze again, keeping it gentle.

"Right. I'll do anything for money." The abashed tone in her voice shouldn't turn me on as much as it does. I love the attitude and her witty remarks, but this is new and so damn hot.

"Safe word." I adjust myself.

"Bells," she answers, shuddering in my hold.

I lean forward, my lips a mere breath away from hers. Her lips purse, but I don't kiss her even though I really want to. "Take your clothes off."

Drawing my hand back, I grab the towel that's wrapped around her head and carefully remove it. I toss it on the coffee table, and her damp hair splays out over her shoulders and down her back.

With her eyes on mine, she grabs the hem of her shirt, pulls it over her head, and drops it on the floor. It's erotic, watching her take every piece of clothing off slowly while I stay where I am, telling her what to do.

Heat floods my body, my cock pulsing and dripping with precum. She stands in front of me naked and fucking perfect. The barbells pierced through her pebbled nipples glint in the light, and goose bumps breakout around the taut skin. Her waist curves in then out to accentuate her wide hips and her thighs. They're thick and muscular, and I want them wrapped around my head.

"Are you not going to take your clothes off?" she asks, gaze coasting over me.

I might've made a mistake because I want nothing more than to drop to my knees and crawl to her. The thought is as invigorating as it is insane.

"No. I want to see you play with yourself." I jump straight into it, desperate to see what she's willing to do and how far I can push. If this is too much, I'll immediately stop, but if it isn't...? Fuck, I might just come in my pants again.

Her eyes go round, mouth opening as if she's going to say something, but she clamps her lips as well as her thighs. Her bright-red toenails curl in and her hands fist at her sides.

"Fingers or toys?" she asks, batting her eyelashes innocently, but I see the wicked way her lips curl.

I adjust myself again, my heart thundering in my chest, picturing her using both. "Just your fingers today." My voice is rough. I clear my throat, but it does nothing for me, not when I have the hottest girl standing in front of me naked.

"And what are you going to do? Just watch me?" She saunters toward me. The heady look in her eyes almost makes me say *fuck this* and just fuck her now, but I tell myself to calm down.

"That's exactly what I'm going to do." I cup her face with both hands. "And you better do a good job because I hate half-assed things."

She heaves a breath. "Could you at least kiss me or touch me?"

I bring my lips to hers, stopping an inch away. "You want that?"

"Yes. Kiss me," she implores, standing on the tips of her toes to connect our mouths, but I jerk back. My eyes are strained from forcing them on her face and not on her tits.

"Beg, then maybe I'll consider it."

She glares but releases a submissive sigh. "Kiss me, please."

Leaning down, I ghost my lips against hers. As her eyes flutter, I drop my hands to her shoulders and spin her around, pinning her back to my chest. I snake my palm around her throat, firmly securing my hold on it and the other on her stomach. I roll my hips, rubbing my cock against her.

"You didn't specify where." Dragging her hair to the left side of her neck, I tip my lips down, nipping and kissing the curve as my hands drift to her stomach down to her pussy. She moans softly then gasps as I slip my fingers between her soaking wet slit.

"Goddamn, Anna." I exhale against her neck, squeezing her throat harder this time. "I told you you'd be wet." I lazily drag my palm over her entire pussy, rubbing her arousal all over it.

"Mmmm." She drops her head on my shoulder, grinding herself on my palm.

"You like that, don't you?" I rasp, adding more pressure but not touching her where I know she wants me to. "You want more?"

"Yes...yes...I need more." She moans a little louder, whining when I remove my hand.

"Good, then you can do it." I push her down onto the sofa, and she brackets her hands on the top backrest. She goes to push up, but I keep a hand on her back, eyes dropping to her round-as-fuck ass. "Goddamn." I cup it, rubbing my palm over her soft cheek before I slap it hard, watching it bounce and turn pink. She jolts then whimpers, dropping her head. I do the same to the other, getting more turned on as I picture her bouncing on my cock. "Play with yourself."

I pull away, sitting down on the coffee table. This angle provides an insane view. I grab myself, feeling my briefs stick to my dick where I've leaked precum. I picture the most degrading things. Anna bent like this while I fuck her. I wonder if she'd be into anal. If she'd let me eat her ass out. I wonder what she'd think of double penetration. My cock in her asshole, dildo rammed deep in her pussy. I wonder so many things, but my perverted thoughts pause when she peers over her shoulder at me. Her gaze flicks down to where my hand is, but I don't move it. I continue to stroke my length.

She goes to move, but I stop her. "No, stay like that. Now hurry the fuck up. It's late and I'm ready to go home."

Her nostrils flare, but those pretty brown eyes flicker with determination. She raises her knees on the couch, hunching forward so her ass lifts, and slips a hand between her thighs. With her eyes still on mine, she drags her middle finger between her slit, moaning when she grazes her clit.

I'm so gone I slip my hand inside my briefs and fist my cock. I drag my fingers over the tip, smearing the precum over it as my gaze bounces between her wet fingers and asshole. It twitches every so often and I wonder if she's thinking what I'm thinking.

Anna wets her lips, eyes trained on my hand now that I pump myself.

"Finger yourself," I rough out, and she does as I instruct, thrusting a finger inside herself. "Shove it as far as it'll go." And again, she does. It's buried knuckle-deep. "Now fuck your finger, roll your hips, make your ass bounce. Show me how badly you want my money." I squeeze myself hard.

She's so obedient, rolling her hips, rocking them back and forth, ass cheeks rippling as she does.

"Add another finger," I order. She drives them as far as she's able to get them and presses the heel of her palm against her clit. She rides the heel of her hand, bucking wildly.

Her moans become breathier, but she wedges her bottom lip between her teeth to muffle the sounds.

"You don't want to be loud, do you?" I grit, and she shakes her head. "You don't want anyone to know why you're doing this." I thrust into my own hand, clenching my teeth as she continues to desperately fuck her fingers. "You don't want them to know you're a slut willing to do anything for money. You don't want them to know that I'm the reason you're greedily fucking your fingers on the sofa, that you get off on this shit. You're so fucking easy. I've got you naked, and I didn't have to beg to get you like this. I can do whatever I want to your—no, to *my* body because your body is mine, right? I fucking own it."

"Shut up. That's not true," she says, looking away, burying her flushed face in the sofa, but I know it's because she's fighting another moan. "You don't—oh fuck." She drops down on her hand and rides it. She's so eager to come, she's frantically moving her hips, rubbing herself on her hand.

"Don't come."

"But I'm so close." She muffles her cries.

"I said don't fucking come, Anna." Pulling my hand out, I stand and fist her hair, yanking her head back. "Don't you dare disobey me. Don't. Come." Dropping her hair, I round the couch, standing in front of her. She lets out a quiet mewling noise, staring up at me with hungry, dazed eyes. "I'm going to help you be quiet, since you're so desperate for it."

A sheen of sweat veils her body, face flushed red. Intrigue sparks in her eyes, but she still continues to work her fingers inside of her, slow and steady. "H-how?" Her eyes flutter closed, and she bites her lip.

I drag my sweats and briefs down and my cock springs free. My head glistens and my shaft is covered in dark, angry veins. She gasps when I fist her hair and yank her head up, eyes bulging. She gapes at my dick, tongue sweeping over her dry lips.

"Stop staring and suck." Jerking her head forward, I grab my length and slap it against her cheek. "Open your mouth and don't stop fucking your hand, but you better not come." I slap the other cheek, enjoying how some of the precum coats her cheeks.

When her lips pop open, I don't waste a second to shove my cock deep inside her hot mouth.

"Fuuuck," I moan, dropping my head back. She gags and chokes a little, but I don't move away. "You wanted to be quiet, you didn't want your neighbors to know how easy you are. You're welcome. Now move your mouth, Anna. I know you're good at this. Don't disappoint me."

I slip out of her mouth, giving her a chance to adjust. She gasps for air, squeezing her eyes shut, but after a second, her lips suction my cock and her cheeks hollow.

"Look at me." I drive it deep, feeling the back of her throat. She gags again but finally looks up at me. Tears prick her eyes, but she doesn't pull away, just greedily sucks in as much air as she can before she goes back to sucking me off while slipping her fingers in and out of herself. "That's it, just like that. I knew you'd be good at this." I draw my gaze down to her heart-shaped ass, picturing the same perverted things I did earlier. I want it so bad.

She moans around me, saliva pooling around her mouth, dripping down her chin and breasts. "You're such a slut for my cock. Just look how well you take me." I thrust deep, holding a firm grip on her hair, keeping her head still and relishing the sound of her gagging. She squeezes her eyes shut, fighting against her reflexes, taking me in and sucking like her life depends on it.

I'm moaning, breathing harshly, my body almost shaking at how she sucks eagerly, like a champ. My balls tighten and a jolt of electricity runs down my body. My dick swells and right as I'm about to burst, I pull out and let my cum shoot all over her face.

My eyes roll back, body sagging forward as I continue to release on her face. I keep one hand around her hair, the other braced on the backrest of the sofa to keep me upright.

"Don't come," I grit.

I think I hear her whine and ask why, but I'm still coming down from my high. I feel so good, my body thrumming with life. I'm so turned on, still hard despite my release. I think about how much I love her mouth and how I desperately want to make every hole in her body mine.

"Sylas, I'm going to come," she cries out, almost screaming from the agony of restraint. I grab the hand she's using and jerk it away.

"I said don't come." I study the cum on her face, feeling feral at the way it drips down and clings to her lips and chin.

She huffs. "Why not?"

"Because I said so." I let go of her hand and grab my shaft. "Looks like you didn't get it all." I peek at the head, eyeing the little bit of cum that still lingers on the tip. "Clean it off."

I draw her face forward, holding my cock close to her mouth. Her jaw tics and fury spikes on her face, but she leans forward and sticks out her tongue. She drags it around my sensitive tip, licking it as if it were an ice cream—with so much vigor. Then she envelops the crown with her mouth, sucking it long and slow, swirling her tongue right on the seam, drawing every last drop.

I clench my teeth, my body tensing from how euphoric she feels. I swear her mouth is magic. I'm practically panting, sweat dripping down my face as my body shivers with ecstasy.

I slump forward when she draws back. "Fucking hell, Anna." I'm winded and exhausted.

"Can I come now?" She places a shaky, wet hand on my forearm, eyes pleading.

I flash her a small, lazy smile and those whiskey eyes bloom with hope. "No."

"Fuck you. I don't have to listen to you."

Letting go of her hair, I carefully lift my sweats and briefs over my hips and grip her chin. "I own your body. I tell you when you can and can't come. If I say no, it means no. Now let's get you cleaned up. I want you to get some rest."

Her brows pinch together. "You just came all over my face. It's not fair that you came and I didn't."

"You're being ungrateful and a fucking brat. Calm down and earn your right to come." I gather the cum on my index finger. "Open your mouth." My cock jerks as she does, and when she sucks my finger clean, I feel myself harden. "Thank me for coming on you."

She scoffs, jerking back. "You're a piece of—"

"Yes, I am, and you'll still thank me. Do it." I look down at her, smirking. It's demeaning, possibly the worst thing I could do after what I did to her face, but all she has to say is "Bells." I wait for the single word to come but she sits up straighter on the couch, swallowing her pride and plastering a smile on her beautiful cum-covered face.

"Thank you for coming on me, Sylas."

I tuck a lock of her hair behind her ear. Wow, she liked this as much as I did. "Are we really doing this?" I soften my voice. "Is this what you like? How you want me to treat you?"

Her eyes level with mine and she smiles coyly. "I like this. I *want* this. I'm okay with it as long as you are."

"I'm great. I'm..." I try to gather my thoughts, still feeling lightheaded from how amazing her mouth felt. "This was...you were incredible."

Her cheeks burn. "I really can't come?"

"No." I grin. "Come on, I'll help you clean up and let you rest."

"You don't have to. I can—"

"Don't fight me on this. I made this mess. I'm going to help you."

"I'm just going to rinse off. I feel so sticky." A drop of cum lands on her lip and she doesn't waste a second to lick it off. Fuck. "I don't need you in the shower with me." She shakes her head as if she could hear my thoughts. "My shower is ridiculously small. There's hardly any space in there for me, so there's definitely not going to be any for you."

"Can I get you anything?" I don't know why I hope she asks me to stay, but when she shakes her head, my stomach dips.

"I'm good. Thanks for everything." Her smile is small and tired. "Good night."

I contemplate asking but decide against it. "Yeah, good night."

16

ANNA

**For the favor.
Do not come.
$5000**

I SQUINT, BRINGING MY PHONE CLOSE TO MY FACE.

My vision is shit and I'm exhausted, which must explain why I'm seeing three zeros next to that five because there is no way Sylas sent me five thousand dollars for a blow job.

But the longer I stare, the more I stop deluding myself.

My jaw drops, but I regret the motion a second later. It sort of aches from the way he fucked my mouth. I was speechless when he pulled his dick out.

The reminder makes my thighs clench, but I don't act upon the impulse of making myself come. Not only when I see the little message he sent along with the money, but because I'm still feeling extremely confused. I decide to call him, assuming he's fucked up the transfer. Maybe he meant to send me fifty dollars or maybe five hundred. The latter is a stretch, but I'm struggling to physically believe he meant to send me that much money for the blow job. Granted, I think I did fantastic, if I do say so myself, and he came on my face.

He answers after the first ring. "Hi, An—"

"I think you made a mistake." I cut him off, burrowing myself deeper in my sheets. "You sent me a lot of money. Too much, actually."

There's a pause on his end, but I know he's there because I hear something rustle in the background. "No, I sent the right amount. Five thousand."

My jaw goes slack, and it still aches, but I can't dwell on that right now.

"Anna, you there?" he asks after a moment, and I realize I've gone seconds, maybe even minutes, without speaking. Stupefaction stole whatever words I had.

"I can't believe I'm saying this." I slip my glasses off and set them on the nightstand. "Five thousand dollars for a blow job? I know I killed it, but that's a lot of money. I probably shouldn't question your generosity. Don't get me wrong, I need the money but...fuck...it's just...I don't know...a lot." I'm stammering, but I can't stop the words from fumbling out of my mouth or what comes out next. "I can't accept it. Five hundred is fine, but take the rest back."

I can't believe I'm saying this. I should happily accept and let it go because stuff like this doesn't ever happen, but it doesn't feel right. I can't believe this is the time I'm choosing to have morals.

"Are you done?" Mirth and indifference coat his words.

"Well...yeah."

"I pay for quality. So, if I gave you that much, it's because it's worth it. Don't question it, and don't start regretting it now. You didn't feel an ounce of guilt when I treated you like a whore, so don't feel bad because I pay you like one." He speaks directly, his words so smug and belittling that I should hate it, but my body reacts so headily, I slip my hand between my thighs. "I hope you're not touching yourself. I didn't give you permission."

My hand freezes and I roll my lips together to hold back my frustrated groan. "You know that's unfair."

"I own your body. At least while we're doing this." He pauses. "I don't understand why you're shocked. I told you it'd be enough for next semester. Keep up, Anna."

I roll my eyes. "I am, and I know."

"Are you still okay with this?" His voice is different than it was a second ago. It's considerate and tentative. Reminding me of the game—the fantasy—we've consented to playing out. "If not, it's strictly fake dating."

"Yes, I'm okay with this." I close my eyes, flustered and embarrassed at how quickly I answered that. I didn't hesitate because I loved the way he used me. It's incredibly degrading, but more than anything, it's exhilarating.

"You have just as much if not more control than I do." His voice is a deep rasp, intensifying the ache between my thighs.

"I don't know...you're the one paying me."

"Doesn't matter. We do as much as you want. We take it as far as you want. We stop whenever you want. You make the decisions."

And that's why it feels exhilarating. It's probably idiotic to blindly hand him over all my trust, but I feel safe with him.

"You know..." I trail off, pausing to figure out how to communicate my jumbled thoughts. "Even without the money, I'd still be okay with this...us."

"Us," he muses, his voice ebbing softly in my ear.

I yawn, blinking the heaviness away from my eyes. "So how does this work?"

"How about we talk later? Text me when you're up? I'll come over."

My heart skips a beat. "Okay."

"Good night, *meu bem*."

My breath catches. "Good night, Sylas." I keep my voice even until I hang up, then a smile so unbearably wide stretches across my face.

What did we just get ourselves into?

17

SYLAS

"OPEN THE DOOR, *MEU BEM*." I RAP MY KNUCKLES ON Anna's apartment door. I attempt to fix the brass number that's crooked on the frame, but it swivels back to how it was originally.

The door opens a sliver, and my fixation on the number and the entire world kind of...fades.

I'm not a saint. I've done my fair share of things, made some choices I'm not proud of, but last night was different. I don't know why, but it was. I keep telling myself it's because of how things played out. How I watched her naked body move, how she rode her fingers, how she took me in her mouth.

But then I think about her smile, like the one she's sporting now. It's small, not reserved but sultry. Amiable. It does the weirdest things to my chest. I don't hyper-fixate on things, but I can feel it; I can see myself obsessing over seeing it.

"Ready to eat?" I hold up the paper bag and cardboard cupholder.

"I can't believe we're doing this." She pulls the door wide open, allowing me to step inside.

"Believe it." I walk past her, hear the door shut, then she's in front of me, guiding me to the living room.

This is my third time in her apartment, and each time I've felt overwhelmed by the decor. It's ridiculous to feel this way over lights and colors, but everything in here feels strangely *real*. There's a warmth to it I can't explain. Which is baffling considering the building and her pint-sized apartment is old and worn down.

She plops down on the sofa, and I settle down next to her. She fixes her attention on our close proximity. After last night, it should be the least of her worries, and because she's going to be my pretend girlfriend, we need to get comfortable sharing space.

"Chai gingerbread latte." I hand her the cup, acting like her fingers brushing against mine didn't make my stomach tighten. I grab my cup and throw the cupholder on the low table. "Don't be weird."

"Thanks, and I'm not being weird." She tucks a leg under her and pushes her glasses up the bridge of her nose. "I'm... processing."

I open the paper bag and hand her her breakfast bagel before grabbing mine. "Well, process faster. We're meeting him today, and I know he's already suspicious this isn't real."

She peers at me, disgruntled. "*Well*, it's not real." She slips her cup between her thighs and pulls back the parchment paper, moaning in appreciation. "But we can make it look real. We just need to be prepared. I don't know how thorough your dad is but—"

"As thorough as Mom." I take a small, careful sip of my black coffee, then nestle the cup between my thighs. "They'll ask questions, like how we met, how long this has been going on, what we plan to make of this. Marriage and—"

"Holy shit." Her jaw drops. "Marriage?" She takes a huge bite of her bagel and chews rather quickly. I stifle a grin. "Your parents are fucking insane. I thought mine were bad. I'm sorry."

"I know." I fold the parchment paper back, blowing on the steaming bagel before taking a bite. I don't know how she didn't burn herself. "And it's fine. They don't expect me to get married now, but they want it to happen with Florence."

She takes another bite, chewing quickly and I watch clouds of steam leave her mouth.

"You're burning the shit out of your tongue. Slow down." I chuckle.

"I like my food really hot. I know it's weird, but if it's not hot, I can't enjoy it."

The way she ate her food fast at Strangers makes sense now. I was too occupied with being in her presence, I didn't put too much thought into it.

"I'll make sure your food stays hot from now on."

"How thoughtful. You already sound like a boyfriend." she sardonically remarks before pushing her glasses up the bridge of her nose. "So, question..."

"Answer."

"Would marrying Florence be such a bad thing?" She eyes me with curiosity. Picking up her cup, she blows faintly through the hole before taking a sip.

I pick at the parchment paper. "Yes. You'd think it'd make sense because we..." I side-eye Anna, who's looking at me like she knows exactly what I'm going to say. I think I see the divot between her brows, but when I really look at her, it's not there.

"Fucked?" She arches her brow.

"Yeah, once." Flashbacks of the night appear in my head. She was angry, but I never found out why. I had my own shit going on, with my father being the cause. We ran into each other, didn't think as we started taking off our clothes, and the rest is hapless history. "Since that night, she's believed we're meant to be."

She hums pensively. "And *that* is why you don't fuck everything you see."

"I saw you at Salt, didn't I?" I flippantly say.

"Oh, get fucked." She laughs and I laugh too. "And that wasn't fucking. We were simply...getting each other off in a way that didn't involve your dick inside of me."

I love how casual and *easy* this feels. I can't remember the last time I had a conversation that didn't revolve around my parents or hockey, and I find myself leaning in, not wanting the moment to end.

"Did it hurt?"

"Did what hurt?"

"Your piercings." I glance at her chest. She's wearing a dark-green oversized pullover that has "Merry Christmas, ya filthy animal" on it.

Anna's gaze follows mine. "Yeah, the second one was a bitch. I think all the adrenaline went to the first and I was slightly in shock from it. So once it wore off, I really felt everything." She peers up at me. "We need to find some common ground. Something that doesn't revolve around our bodies and sex. We're good at that, but I don't think your parents would appreciate it."

I snicker, taking another bite, and nod. "We have it."

"What is it?"

"This—how easy everything is between us. How we align so well and maybe in a strange way, make a lot of sense together." I falter, realizing it sounds cliché, but there's no point taking it back. I meant what I said. "We didn't know each other a couple weeks ago and now look at us. I'm sure my parents have their doubts, but we'll sell it."

She goes quiet and I wonder if what I said sounds ridiculous. I don't know where it came from, but it made sense. Like we do. I don't understand it, but it's comforting being around her. Whether it involves being physical or not.

Her lips curl into a...*bashful*...smile? And her eyes soften, alight with a tenderness.

I don't know what classifies as a crush, but maybe Thea and Marc are right. Maybe that's what this is.

Why is it so hard to know?

She looks away and picks up her cup, taking a drink. "So... um..." she stammers, tucking a lock of her hair behind her ear that's covered in piercings. "What do you think they'll expect to see from us? Do we need to be affectionate? Or..."

Anna and I stand outside Linked, the restaurant my parents chose. She looks up at me and I down at her. She doesn't appear nervous, but still I check in.

"Nervous?" I hold my hand out. "Not regretting it are you?"

She slips her hand in mine, and when I squeeze it, she squeezes back. "No. Not nervous. Like you said, this, us, feels easy. I don't know how to make sense of it either, but I'm okay. Are you nervous?"

"No." *Yes*, but only because this could go sideways in seconds. Mom will be cordial; Dad, I don't know. I drum my fingers in my pocket, desperately craving a cigarette since I don't have gum right now. "Thanks for letting me drag you into the bullshit mess I call my family. On the positive side, my sister is nice."

She chuckles. "Great, I can take your parents despising me, but I don't know if I'd be okay with my *sister-in-law* hating me."

My lips twitch, and the noose of anxiety wrapped around my neck loosens. Leave it to her sarcasm to make me feel at ease. "Let's go inside. They're already here, waiting for us."

As I usher her inside and the hostess leads us to the table, I think to myself how crazy this all is. Is this really necessary so my parents can stop pushing for Florence and me to happen? One look at Anna and I immediately think *yes*.

I kind of hate that I dragged her into this, but...I also don't. I'll keep that to myself because how do I explain that I'm really enjoying this?

Who would've thought I'd be okay holding hands with a girl?

When my parents come into view, Anna straightens. I squeeze her hand, and she squeezes back.

Here goes nothing.

18

ANNA

Sunday, December 15

I MAY HAVE OVERESTIMATED MY ABILITY TO REMAIN calm.

I am, in fact, freaking out.

Outside, I was fine, and having Sylas at my side made me feel mellow. But now, my nerves are coiled tight.

I've dealt with the rich for years, so it should be straightforward, but this is different to working for them. This is sharing a meal and getting judged, because I just know his parents will.

This is pretend, I remind myself. It's not like I'll have to put up with them forever. I just need to smile and sell the hell out of our fake relationship.

Happy, obsessed, and in love, I chant in my head. No, wait, maybe *in love* is pushing it, but we're in a relationship, so we're supposed to come off that way, right?

This is pretend. Happy, obsessed, and in love.

"Anna, we're so glad you were able to join us." His mom stands, and the overzealous energy she radiates throws me off, but I'm astonished when she tugs me in for a hug and gives me a faux kiss on the cheek.

"Thank you for inviting me, Mrs. Lenoir." I smile at her when she draws back. She kept her maiden name, Alves, but I wasn't sure whether to add that too or not.

"Oh please, call me Clara."

"If you insist."

"I do." She beams, her pearly white teeth glowing.

Sylas studies her with apprehension before welcoming her hug with a kiss on the cheek. Then his father stands and extends his hand for me to take.

"Anna." He doesn't smile but he doesn't stare at me the way he did at the auction.

"Mr. Lenoir." My smile lifts higher. I know his name—Dean—but I'm not sure if I should call him by it, and I have my answer when he doesn't correct me.

"Hey, I'm Thea," his sister says from her chair, offering me a nod. Everything about her expression feels forced. Even the way she's sitting looks stiff.

"Anna, but you already know that." Still, I keep my lips curled, and hopefully everything about me screams I'm cool, calm, and confident.

Once we take our seats and order our drinks, the table goes tensely quiet.

Sylas is the first to speak. "Don't do this. You have us here. Whatever you're going to ask, just ask it."

Oh my god. I'm not sure if I should duck and expect some kind of lash-out that will lead to the argument of the year, so I hold my breath as I wait.

My parents thrive off confrontation, especially my mother. She has a comeback for everything and no matter what, she's never wrong. They always made me nervous and I always avoided them because they would lead to hour-long lectures. To her, it was never an argument; to her, it was just us talking.

I'd avoid them at all costs, especially because her passive-aggressiveness was sometimes too much to handle. Occasionally, I could put up with certain things, but her belittling remarks were hard to let slide.

"We're just having dinner," Clara starts.

Thea's gaze slips between each family member, but she stays quiet. She looks between bored and annoyed, though I'm not sure which.

Sylas levels his mom with a suspicious look. "So, we're just here for dinner?"

"Yes, Sylas," his dad answers, a little irritated at him before his deep British voice becomes indifferent. "We're just having dinner with your girlfriend, who we didn't know existed until a few days ago."

"We told you it's new," Sylas adds.

"We're still getting to know one another," I insert, not sure if I should've said anything at all.

"Right." There's something sardonic about the way he said that single word. But it's the slight twist of his lips and spark of challenge in his eyes that make me uncomfortable. "With that being said, because this is *new*, has Sylas already told you how devoted he is to hockey? Because if he hasn't, I need you to know that it *has* and *will* always come first. Everything is either second or last in his life. I need you to understand that he can't afford distractions. Isn't that right, Sylas?" he states, directing his intense, hardened eyes at him.

"That's—"

"I can't afford distractions either." I talk over Sylas, and they all turn to stare at me like I've said something otherworldly. "What I mean is, I have a lot going on in my life. Sylas knows that, just like I know he has a lot going on as well. Which is why we're taking things slow, getting to know one another."

His father hums, and he scrutinizes me. "What is it you do?"

Sylas places his hand on my thigh, squeezing it gently as if he were trying to reassure me that it's all going to be okay. "I'm a full-time student. I have two jobs and run my own business."

"What kind of business?" Clara asks, eyes sparkling.

"Baking. I bake all sorts of things," I answer proudly.

"She's really good. She has this Instagram page of all the stuff she's made," Sylas adds, just as proud.

I can't mask my shock quick enough, but once I recover a second later, I hide it. I didn't know he had looked at my page.

"Oh, cute." Clara grins, but the sound and expression of her flawless, wrinkle-free face feels and looks fake. It's condescending and placating. I know it well—Mom adopted a similar one when I wore something she wasn't a fan of.

Sylas removes his hand off my thigh and grabs mine, placing it on the table. Everyone's gaze lands on it.

It's intimate, the way he carefully holds it, how he rubs his thumb soothingly over my knuckles. For never having had a girlfriend, he's good at this. Even the way he holds my stare feels personal, affectionate, *special*.

"I don't understand why this relationship is necessary if you're both immensely busy?" his father voices, breaking the spell we're in.

For a mere second, I genuinely forgot they were here.

"We like each other," Sylas answers, but his eyes are on mine, full of warmth as his dimples indent each cheek. My stomach rampantly flutters. "It's not like we're getting married or putting anything on hold to be with each other." He now looks at them with a forced friendliness. "We're taking things slow, but we're exclusive. I don't want anyone else and neither does Anna, so here we are." He raises our joined hands as if to prove a point.

They're not convinced. At least his dad isn't. Thea looks like she couldn't care less, and his mom looks like she either supports us or is having a heart attack. I don't know what to make of Clara, but something is off about her. However, she's the least of my worries because his father is staring at me like I'm the gum beneath his shoe.

But it's a short-lived look because he smiles. Granted, it's tight, but I'll take it. "Well, Anna, we're happy to have you here."

His words sound robotic, like it took everything in him to voice them out loud.

"Thanks for having me." I make sure my smile doesn't mirror his, and keep it firmly in place throughout dinner.

In spite of it all, Sylas makes a pretty good boyfriend. I know he's doing his best to sell this relationship, but I swear at times it feels...real.

19

SYLAS

I'M GOING THROUGH GUM FASTER THAN I'VE EVER GONE through anything in my life. Every time I think of reaching for a cigarette, I grab a stick or cube of gum.

I bought a variety because some aren't as good as they're advertised, and some, while good, don't last in flavor. And sometimes, depending on the day or what my father says, I'll need something strong. Unfortunately, gum isn't known for being *strong* in nerve-shattering abilities.

I miss my cigarettes. The stupid withdrawal is giving me horrible headaches, and everything annoys the shit out of me.

Popping in a minty cube, I push the button on my lighter down and keep my eyes trained on the elevator.

I had practice with my father early this morning, followed by drills with the guys, and then met my father again to review film.

He was his usual asshole self, but something was different.

I waited for him to talk about Anna, expected it to happen —mentally prepared myself, even—but the questions never came. It's strange, but it's the least of my problems. My shoulder started acting up. I couldn't think of anything but making sure I didn't strain it and prayed it didn't pop out of place again.

I chew fast, my jaw becoming sore, but I don't let up nor do I stop playing with the lighter.

Knowing Anna is coming today is the only thing keeping me from going mental. She somehow helps slow my quick-paced thoughts. I don't know what it is about being with her, but she makes me feel at ease.

So much so that when I hear the elevator door ping, I stop playing with the lighter, my jaw relaxes, and my chewing is steady.

She strolls out of the elevator with a cart full of cleaning supplies by herself.

Anna's got her earbuds in so she doesn't notice me at first, head bobbing to the Christmas song playing. It's loud, and I make out Mariah Carey's distinct voice.

I wave my hand, loudly calling her name, but she's oblivious, head still bobbing, two buns on her head moving as she sings along.

When she finally turns around, she gasps and drops a bright yellow rag on the floor.

"What the hell, Sylas?" she squeaks, removing her earbuds.

I snicker, sauntering over to her, and pick up the rag. "I tried to get your attention."

She peers up at me, a deep frown on her face. "By standing there like a creep? You could've come up to me."

I shrug, shaking the rag for her to take, but she doesn't. "Not a creep. It's my home. I can stand wherever I want, and I didn't want to get in your way."

"So, what? You're saying it's my fault?"

"Yeah, you being easily spooked is your fault. But if I apologize, will you stop being mad at me?" I smile at her but then can't help but laugh.

"What's so funny?" Her hardened expression softens, and she chuckles a little.

"This feels like déjà vu..."

She has this faraway look on her face, but a second later, it dawns on her. "A creep then, a creep now. Some things don't change."

I'm taken aback and tighten my hold on the rag as she tries to yank it free. "It's not my fault you didn't notice me both times. It's important to be aware of your surroundings." I blatantly let my eyes drift down her body. She's wearing her cleaning service outfit, a black collared shirt with *Elite Housekeeping* sewn in gold thread on the top right of her breast, and black joggers. "And I'm not sorry for checking you out." I wasn't actually; I was too busy feeling relieved that she's here. "I've seen you naked and you're really pretty, so sue me."

Her chest expands, a small divot nestles between her brows, and the apples of her cheeks flush. She glances at her cart, brushing her bangs away from her forehead, but they fall back to where they were originally.

I smirk then blow a bubble.

"How's the gum?" she asks, eyes on my mouth.

I blow another bubble, tugging the rag so she steps closer to me. "It's...minty."

"You hate it, don't you?" She asks, amused, letting me pull until the front of her shoes hit mine and our fingers brush.

"It's...growing on me..." I blow another one, but she pops it this time. I stick my tongue out to clean it off my lips, and her eyes follow the movement.

"I can tell." With her free hand, reaches up to my face, but she doesn't touch me. "You have—"

"Go ahead." I lean down, holding my breath when her cold finger brushes the corner of my mouth to remove the remnants of the gum I didn't get. She rubs firmly but slowly, and despite her skin freezing, it sears me.

My heart skips a beat, my jaw aches, and I notice how hard I'm clenching my teeth. I swallow and chew, realizing I had stopped doing that.

"Got it." She removes the rag from my hand, wipes her finger on it, and takes a few steps back.

"Thanks. Best girlfriend ever." I wink at her.

She blushes. "You make a corny boyfriend."

"Isn't that the whole point?"

"I don't know, I guess." She shrugs, gaze sweeping over me in a thoughtful way.

"What?" I watch her the same way she's looking at me.

It's beyond me how good this—*we* work. How we make sense and everything feels steady when I'm around her. It's also pretty crazy how much I like being around her and how I look forward to this—*her*.

Is this what a crush does to you? Makes your heart palpitate out of control, hands clammy, thoughts racing—not in an anxious kind of way but in a way you want to talk about everything and anything and you're not sure where to start?

Then there's looking forward to the small things, like hoping her eyes are always on me, wanting to touch her because I just need to feel her skin. Seeing red tint her cheeks and knowing I'm the reason for it.

But is this considered a crush? Is this not too soon? Is this sane? Am *I* sane?

Should I consult my therapist for this? I haven't spoken to him in a while; surely, he'll know what's going on, right?

Her lips tug into a pretty smile. "For never being a boyfriend, you're good at this. You were phenomenal yesterday. If hockey doesn't work out, you should consider acting."

I'm not sure how much my parents are sold on this, but Thea said she'd have believed it, if she didn't already know it was fake. Mom didn't ask questions, only texted me and said it's a pity it didn't work with Florence, but she's willing to give Anna a chance.

She's taking this better than I expected. But I'm not naive to believe she's suddenly changed. Something's different, I just don't know what.

And going into acting? Mom would love that since she's a director and her side of the family is all part of that industry.

I grin and lift my shoulder in an absent shrug. "It's hard to fake something that feels natural. I just...I don't know...did what felt right. Hard to explain but—"

"No, I get it. It felt—*feels*...good. *We* did good. If you ever need a girlfriend, you can hit me up." She makes a phone sign with her hand, placing it by her ear. "*Call me, beep me, if ya wanna reach me,*" she singsongs.

I chuckle. "Where's that from?"

She stares at me, bewildered. "Do you not know who the *Kim Possible* is?"

I ponder it, but nothing comes to mind. "No? Am I supposed to?"

"Oh God, I'm breaking up with you." She looks so offended it's cute.

"You can't. Not until the end of the semester. Until then, you're stuck with me, *meu bem*." I wonder what her being stuck with me this semester will look like?

Her eyes level with mine, and for a second, I wonder...is she thinking it too?

"Well then, as my boyfriend"—*yeah, I like the sound of that*—"you'll have to watch it with me. No ifs, ands, or buts. Got it? Good talk. I need to clean."

Anna tries to walk around me, but I grab her forearm and stop her, but then I drop it, realizing it's the arm she got the tattoo on. "How's your arm?"

"Sore. I still can't believe we did that."

I glance at my covered arm then back at her. "Believe it because we did and it'll be on you forever."

"I'm just glad it's cute and not something ugly or ridiculous like a jellyfish."

"Hey." I feign offense. "They happen to be really fucking cute."

She laughs and I do too. "Yeah, I guess they are." She holds my stare and suddenly everything is white noise and nothing matters. It's just her and me. This feels good. "I really need to clean now."

"I already did it."

"What?" She's staring at me, unblinking and shocked. "You did what?"

"I cleaned. You're my girlfriend," I start. "It doesn't feel right that you're cleaning my place and—"

"I'm not *really* your girlfriend, and I get paid to do this, Sylas."

There's an ugly dip in my stomach. "I know we're not real, but it still doesn't feel right. So don't worry about it. Although it definitely doesn't look anywhere as good as you do, but it's clean and that's good enough for me."

She still looks stunned but recovers. "I really need this job. If I'm not cleaning and Michael finds out, I'll get fired."

"Then don't tell him. I won't. What he doesn't know won't hurt him."

"Your parents pay him to pay me. This doesn't—"

"Money is the least of my parents' worries." I realize how pompous that sounds, but it's the truth. There's no point in downplaying it. "Don't worry about it. I'm not going to tell them. Either way, this is my home. What I decide to do with it is on me."

She looks uncertain.

"I swear, the last thing I want to do is get you in trouble."

Anna's still quiet, so without thinking I grab her hand in mine like I did yesterday. She doesn't jerk it away, so I think that's a good sign.

"Let's pretend."

"Hmm?"

I rub circles on her now warm hand. "This...us. Let's pretend it's real. That we are in a relationship and because we are in one that means we need to have trust. So trust me. No one has to know what we do." I inch closer, tucking the long piece of her bang behind her ear. "Either way, everyone already thinks we're in one. So let's pretend we are."

"Sy—Sylas," she stammers, smiling disbelievingly.

"I know it sounds crazy, but just think about it. We can make it work."

Anna mulls it over, sucking her bottom lip into her mouth. "I don't know...do you think we can really play pretend? What if you get tired of me? Or what if I get tired of you? Or what if—"

"What if this all works out? It's just pretend, and once the semester is over, we'll mutually split. Come on, Anna, let's pretend."

"I-I really don't know..." She clicks her tongue.

"Let's do a little trial."

She chuckles. "A trial?"

"A *Christmas* trial. We'll see how things play out this month. If everything works out, we keep it up, and if things don't, then we don't." It sounds really stupid when I think about it, but what's the worst that's going to happen? I'll fall in love?

No, that'd be too soon. I don't understand a crush, so how would I understand what love is?

She tips her head back, a full laugh expelling from her mouth. I can't help but take her in and appreciate how fucking beautiful she is.

"You'd really be exclusive to me for the rest of the semester? No having sex with other girls? No flirting? No nothing? Because if you still want to, we can fake it in front of your parents, but—"

"No. None of that. I swear." I earnestly reply, hoping she believes me because I'd never do anything to break her trust or hurt her.

She studies it and exhales a deep sigh. "Sy—ahhh...fuck it. Okay. What's the worst that could happen?"

"That's the spirit." I'm fucking beaming. I've never been this elated in December. "I'm not trying to be a control freak, but I don't want you to be—"

She scowls. "I'm your girlfriend. I only want *you*."

Anna only wants me. God, I'm so obsessed with the sound of that.

My heart races. "Right, yeah. Just making sure we're on the same page."

She's grinning now. "We are. You really don't want me to clean?"

I look over my shoulder. "Nah." Then I peer down at her.

"So...now what?"

"Do you know how to skate?"

20

ANNA

"You promise you won't let me fall?" I glance hesitantly at the glistening iced floor, then at the people who swiftly and deftly skate in circles.

Sylas grabs my hands, softly squeezing and tugging them to get me to look up at him. A beguiling smile curls his lips, his dimples denting his cheeks. "Do you not know who you're skating next to? You're in the greatest hands."

"So what...you like...skate or something?" I satirically say, the nerves lessen at the unimpressed expression on his face. "You're already conceited enough as it is. Someone has to keep your ego in check."

"Ha ha, funny." He grins. "I promise you'll be okay."

We came to Wollman Rink in Central Park. Because it's still very early, a little past noon, there's not a lot of people, and the sun is brightly shining down on us. It shouldn't be too bad, but I've never been the strongest skater. I've ice skated before, but it's been a while, and when I did, I was either holding hands with Jenny or holding on to the railing for support.

He steps on the ice, standing comfortably and steadily while he guides me to follow behind him until I'm also on the ice. My feet slip beneath me, but Sylas keeps his hands firm on me, until the blades stop skidding on the ice.

"You're okay, I've got you." He twines his fingers through my cold ones. "Don't tense up. Just relax and follow my lead. I promise you'll be okay."

And I do, not easily, but he holds me, effortlessly and slowly —for my sake—as he leads me along the sleek ice.

Beams of light reflect off it onto his face, making his already sparkling smile burn bright. "Just look at you. You're a natural."

I test out a smile. "You don't have to be nice. I'm shit. Those littles kids over there"—I tip my head in the direction of the boys who look like they're eleven and skating with ease—"have skated laps around us. *Laps*," I emphasize.

"You want me to trip one of those little shits for you?"

I laugh, shaking my head at the serious tone in his voice. They did almost run into us a few times and have been little shits, but they're kids and there's policemen around. "No...or maybe when no one is looking."

"Okay." He winks at me. It should be illegal how ridiculously ethereal his green eyes look beneath the sun. They're pale but translucent and airy.

"So..." I begin, gliding more comfortably on the ice. "Why do they call you the Punisher? Does the fight have something to do with it?"

He laughs, dimples on display. "You looked me up?"

I shrug, not meeting his stare. I had before but not like last night where I spent an insane amount of time searching him up. "I figured if we're going to fake it, I'll need to know more about you. Your parents didn't ask a lot of questions, but I'm sure they will eventually."

That's a lame response and I know Sylas thinks just as much because he scoffs. "You just wanted to look me up, didn't you?"

My lips tick up a little. "Shut up. It's not—"

"Bullshit." He speaks over me. "Did you watch my highlights?"

Loved seeing me in my uniform? Get turned on by it? Did you replay the clips?"

Now I scoff, loud enough that the people next to us skate past us, peeping at us. "Sylas, you are—" I chuckle in astonishment. "There are not enough words to describe what you are. There are enough self-important people in this city. There's not enough room for you here. So stop—"

"I can't. I won't." He raises my hand and shocks me when he brings it to his mouth and brushes his lips along my knuckles. His breath tickles and warms my cold skin. "I can't help it, I'm an assured person," he says as he drops my hand, still keeping a firm hold on it.

He did it so absently, like it was something he didn't think about. Something he did, just to do. Something he's done countless times.

It's bizarre—in a good way—how *pretending* feels so real.

"*Assured,*" I mock, watching the white cloud of my breath get carried away by the chilly wind. "*Bigheaded* suits you better."

A haughty smirk stretches across his face. "But really, you looked me up?"

Flashbacks of last night's videos surface. His agility, his speed, his strength, the way he carries himself. I see why he's so proud. He's good, although saying *good* is probably downplaying how talented he is.

"Yes, happy? You're my boyfriend. I feel like I still don't know a lot about you, and I was thinking of your parents. Eventually, they'll ask me questions."

And maybe I looked him up just to see him in his uniform.

"Whatever you want to know, just ask. If you want pictures or videos, I'm happy to send those to you. All you have to do is ask, *girlfriend.*"

I chuckle and pause, my gaze gravitating toward the orange cones placed on the ice in the center. There's a girl, who I assume is a figure skater because she jumps and twirls so effortlessly.

"I'll pass." I grin at the playful roll of his eyes. "So, why 'Punisher'?"

"I watch an episode of *The Punisher* before every game."

"Superstitious much?" I tease.

"Don't judge me. I have to. If I don't, I'm thrown off my game." He smiles, knowing I mean nothing by it. "I also have tea and eat a peanut butter and jelly sandwich before every game."

I did know that, and I think it's cute. "Why *The Punisher* though?"

"Because the first time I watched it before a game, I scored a hat trick and the one time I didn't watch it, my shoulder popped out of its socket." There's a grim look on his face, jaw tense before he blinks and it's gone. "Sorry about our communications class—"

"It's fine. I'm over it. How's your shoulder now?" I glance at it, remembering how he stood after he was harshly shoved against the boards then dropped to the ground, holding his arm.

"It's good." But he doesn't sound sure of himself like he usually does. "Never been better."

I stare skeptically at him. He looks out of it, like he's not himself.

"Are you sure?"

His smug smile returns. "Positive. I'm good. That was three years ago. As was the fight." He sighs sharply, and a billowing white cloud expels from his mouth.

The change of conversation screams he's done talking about it. I want to let him know he can talk to me, but this is fake, after all. He doesn't necessarily have to tell me anything. Although I do want to know, I'm not sure how much I can ask or what I can ask. I don't want to make him uncomfortable.

Still, I say, "If you ever want to talk about it, I'm here, fake girlfriend or not."

"I love how much you care about me." He kisses my knuckles again, making my stomach flutter.

"Don't let it go to your head," I say, then playfully swat him away.

"The moment all of this started, anything you have done or said has gone straight to my head." The deep, heated look in his eyes makes my heart rattle and my face warm despite the brittle air.

"So…" I can't think straight. I will my heart to slow down. "All jokes aside, I'm here. I'm serious. If you want to talk about it or about anything else, I'm here."

He stares at me for a long beat, his eyes softening, but there's a heaviness behind them. But once he blinks, they're vibrant and his lips are stretched up again. "Yeah. So what were we talking about again?"

I wish I could say something else, but I know he's done. So I let it go, even though I really don't want to.

"The fight. Why? And how much trouble did you get in? I read you're not allowed to fight per the NCAA rules."

"Just how much did you research?" He smiles wide, voice knowing.

"I got a hockey skate tattooed on my arm. I might as well know what all the hype is about. I still don't think I understand it, but it's cool."

"That's fair." Sylas laughs. "I was ejected, got my ass handed to me by Coach and my father, but it was worth it. There's so much you can do and I'll let slide, but no one fucks with Thea."

"One of the players was talking about your sister?"

"Yeah." His jaw tics. "Apparently, he had asked her out, she turned him down, and that's when he started running his mouth."

"And people say women are emotional," I state derisively. "And that's without a period. Now imagine if men had periods."

His lips twitch, but then his nose scrunches in a grimace.

"Don't tell me you're one of those."

"One of what?"

"Periods gross you out?"

"No, I have a sister who on occasion lacks a filter. Especially when she's on her period. Everything is my fault and men are shit." His tone is grave, but he smiles, nonetheless.

"I like her, but I think she might hate me."

"Thea? No. She knows about us. She's a little prickly and looks serious most of the time, but I swear she's sweet when she wants to be."

My brows arch in surprise. "You told her about us?"

There's a tint of pink on his cheeks. I can't tell if they're a little brighter because of the frosty air or because he's blushing.

"She would've asked regardless. Plus, I trust her."

"You two are close?"

He nods. "Yeah, we get along. Growing up, we didn't, but we're good now."

A knot grows in the middle of my throat. I say nothing, afraid my jealousy will sneak past my mouth and dampen the mood. I'm not close with Maya. I tried, I really did, but our lives are different, and she didn't support my needs and wants despite how much I've supported her.

"She also plays hockey, right?"

"Yeah, and she swears she's better than me." He snickers. "Don't let her con you into believing that."

I grin. "Have you guys always played?"

"For as long as I can remember, I have. Thea was a figure skater at one point, but she got a feel of the puck, the stick, the adrenaline, and converted. Mom was angry but eventually got over it." He rolls his eyes.

"Our parents could be best friends," I joke, and it eases the tension on his face.

"They'd get along well, huh?"

If it weren't because they're in different tax brackets, I'm sure his parents would get along just fine with mine.

"You know, I've never seen *The Punisher*."

He dramatically gasps. "Anna, baby"—*baby*...Why do I like the sound of that?—"I know what we're doing tonight."

I giddily smile. "Not tonight."

"You've got plans?" he nonchalantly asks, but I hear the curiosity in his voice.

"No, I work at the restaurant. And after, I'm calling Jenny."

"She didn't come to work with you today? Or the other day... Does that happen a lot?"

"Her grandma is sick; I told her to go be with her. We always cover for each other whenever something is going on. Michael's strict about us calling out and I can't say I blame him, considering who his clientele is," I explain. "Anyway, we're always checking in with each other."

He hums. "You guys are really close, huh?"

"She's my best friend and the closest thing I have to family around here."

I feel his gaze burn the side of my face, the sympathy oozing off him. "Do you not plan to go back home to visit your family?" he asks carefully.

"No, my parents are mad, and my sister is on their side. Most of my other family members will either side with them or say nothing, but things will be awkward, nonetheless, so I'd rather not go home."

Not sure if I should even call it "home" because unless things somehow magically work out between us, I don't see myself going back.

"You want to spend it with me?" he asks.

The cloud of sadness dwindles. "With your parents? Will they be okay with that?"

"They will for the party they're throwing on Christmas Eve. It's over the top and everyone will be there. And now that you're my girlfriend, I'm sure they'll expect for you to be there. I didn't think to ask you. So much has been—"

"I get it." I smile at him. "I'll be there if you want me there."

"I do. I really do." There's an urgency in his voice.

"Then I'll be there. How...extravagant is this party?"

"Very, but don't worry about your dress. We can pick something up together. Whenever you have time."

"I can wear the one—"

At the shake of his head, I snap my mouth shut.

I know what the shake means. I can't show up wearing a dress I already wore.

That's insane, but I don't question it.

"My mom, she's particular. She'll talk about it for months to come." He groans, frowning.

I laugh. "Don't worry. I don't mind dressing up."

Relief washes over him. "But on Christmas Day, we can do our own thing. Though first thing in the morning, I'll have to go over for a little bit. Take pictures with them so they can post to their socials and do all that bullshit. I'd invite you, but trust me, you don't want to be there." I don't miss the indignation in his voice. "But afterward, I'm all yours. I don't ever do anything, so you can pick what we do."

"You're not a fan of Christmas, are you?" I shiver a little as the wind gets stronger.

He notices and guides me to the exit.

"How'd you guess?" Sylas says sardonically.

"In all the years I've cleaned your home, you've never had any decorations up. And you...I don't know. It seems like it's an inconvenience to you."

I sit at a bench, and he kneels down.

My heart takes flight the same way it did earlier when he offered to help me put on my skates and tie them for me. It's unnecessary, really, but there's a softness in his smile, a warmth in his eyes that makes me shudder. Not because I'm cold, but because I'm burning in a way that makes all these layers of clothes unbearable.

"You really don't have—"

"I want to. Let me," he implores gently, his eyes a sharp green color like two pools of emeralds. They're pretty, hard to look away from, hard to say no to.

"Okay." I feel shy, I don't know why. He's doing something nice, but it's intimate. The way he loosens the strings, makes sure my foot doesn't touch the ground. His hands, despite their size, hold my foot with so much care and consideration it makes the burn inside magnify. He makes me feel like I'm something precious to him.

My stomach somersaults and I have to remind myself to focus on his lips moving and the words coming out of his mouth.

"I don't hate the holiday itself I guess...my parents...they make it about them. It's all fake—everything we do, how we do it. The constant smiles, pretending to like everyone, getting along with everyone, pleasing everyone, it gets tiring."

It's no different than what we're doing, I want to say. And it's like he knows what I'm thinking because he looks up at me.

"I'm not tired of this, Anna. I like this," he assures me, his voice decisive like it's not something he needed to think about or say to placate me. "Believe me?"

"I do." And I mean it.

"Let's hurry and get you warmed up."

21

SYLAS

> Berlin: When the fuck were you going to tell us
> you have a girlfriend? A GIRLFRIEND!!!!
>
> Frost: Anna Lopez?? The girl from Salt. The
> girl who bid on you?? There's no way she
> agreed to be with you of all people.
>
> Berlin: Does she know she's your girlfriend?
>
> Frost: Poor thing. She was probably coerced.
> How'd you do it, Sy? How'd you get her to
> agree to put up with you?

SINCE THE GUYS FOUND OUT ABOUT ANNA, THEY'VE been asking questions nonstop. I've been ignoring them because I didn't really know what to say.

Everything was supposed to stop at the auction, then I lied and it evolved into more. Marc knows everything, as does my sister, but that's as many people as I want knowing.

I could tell the guys—I trust them, but I know Frost is interested. I don't care what he says or how he tries to downplay it, since the night at Salt, he's had his eye on her. Frost is a good guy, but he's also an opportunist. I know the moment he finds out it's fake, he'll reach out and shoot his shot. And Berlin, he's close to Frost, like I'm close with Marc.

Though I shouldn't be worried, because we're "dating" whether or not my parents are around. That sounds ridiculous, and in some way, complicated—like Marc and Thea implied the other day.

I know I'm being a little bitch by not forwardly asking Anna if she wants to give this a shot. It's obvious we're into each other. It's obvious something is there. I can't ignore the way my heart, mind, and body react and gravitate toward her whenever she's around.

I kept telling myself it wasn't a crush because I've never had one, never felt one, never cared for anyone, but I knew it was real when my first thought this morning wasn't hockey but Anna. I thought about how she'd come over today and how I cleaned and felt I did better than last time. I wondered what earrings she'd wear because every time I see her, she has a different pair on. If she'll wear contacts or glasses. If she'll have her hair up or down or in those space buns.

I keep wondering about things I never did before, craving them even. Things that before Anna were inconsequential to me.

But despite the obvious sexual tension, because there's a lot of that, I don't know for sure if Anna *likes* me.

I could ask but if she says no, it'll make things weird, and weird is not something I need.

So if pretending is as good as it'll get, then so be it.

> Me: I'm not sure why you're all surprised. You've seen what I look like. Anna liked what she saw, no coercion on my end. I know it's something you're used to doing, Frosty, but I didn't have to manipulate someone into being with me.

> Frost: You pretentious piece of shit. Get fucked

Berlin: Sy, I've seen you. You're not all that

Me: I'm here for the bromance. Berlin, your allegiance to Frosty is cute.

Marc: I've got nothing to say. I'm just here for the entertainment

Frost: Be serious, Sy. We know you don't do monogamy. Pretty sure you're allergic to it, and you probably didn't know the word existed until today. Are you using Anna to avoid Florence?

Me: Is it really hard to believe I developed feelings?

Berlin: Yes. I'm surprised you know what they are

Frost: I'm surprised you have them for someone that isn't yourself

I roll my eyes as I contemplate what to say.

Marc: He got jealous when Alex tried to ask her out. So the feelings are there

I know he thinks he's helping, but I wish he hadn't told them that. I'm not a jealous person and I don't want them to know or use her to get under my skin. Despite being my friends, they can be assholes when they want to be.

Frost: The world is ending. Sylas Lenoir Alves jealous? No way

Berlin: No, it did happen. Alex was bitching about him. Now it makes sense. You got jealous? Damn. The world is ending. We're fucked.

> Me: Berlin, fuck you. Everett, you never had a chance with her. Piss off. Marc, shut up. Rowan, fuck you for never saying anything or having my back.

He's in the group chat but never answers. Pretty sure he has our chat on silent.

It's childish, but I leave the group chat. A second later, Marc adds me back to it.

Rolling my eyes, I slip my phone in my pocket, swapping it for my lighter. I pick up the gum from the island, grab two minty cubes, pop them in my mouth, and stand by the elevator, waiting for Anna.

I chew hard. My jaw starts to hurt, but I don't let up. I play with the lighter, watching the flame rise then die out until I repeat the motion again. My head hurts, my shoulder feels tight, and I'm annoyed.

I want a cigarette, but I want Anna more.

Checking the time, I see more messages pop up, but I ignore them and draw my gaze back to the elevator.

Right on time, a soft ping echoes, the doors slide open, and Anna walks out by herself with her cart full of supplies, earbuds blaring Christmas music in her ears.

Her hair is up in a ponytail, she's wearing these gold Christmas tree earrings and the others are small studs or hoops, she has her contacts on, and she's in her uniform.

But unlike the other few times I caught her off guard gasping and staring at me wide-eyed, this time she pops out an earbud and lifts a brow, staring at me as if she were asking *What are you doing here?*

"Don't look at me like that," I chastise. "I live here, or did you forget? But let's not talk about me right now. What are you doing here...wearing that?"

She watches me, dumbfounded, and takes the other earbud

out. "Working. You know that. I come here every Monday, Wednes—"

"Anna. *Meu bem*. Baby." I wipe a palm down my face. "You're *my* girlfriend." I emphasize. "*We* said you wouldn't do this anymore." I inch closer until she's craning her neck to look up at me. "We're still pretending, aren't we?"

I think she's wearing makeup because her lashes are thicker, darker, and there's a glimmer that reflects from her lids. Her usual pink lips are slightly glossy, and she smells good, though she usually does, but it's different.

She offers me a tight-lipped smile. "Yes, we're still pretending, but I figured maybe I should still come and clean."

"Why?" I absently reach for her hand, and when my finger brushes her arm, I hear her breath hitch.

"Because..." Her voice is softer now. "Getting paid for not doing anything feels wrong. And either way, I need to deep clean."

"I've cleaned. Not sure what you mean by *deep clean*, but I thoroughly cleaned." I grin at the shock on her face and hook a finger around hers. "I did look up YouTube videos because I had no idea how or where to begin. But you don't have to worry about anything. As for feeling bad, stop it. Don't."

"You looked up videos?" Her jaw falls slack and she looks around me. "What did you clean with? How did you clean? When did you—"

I can't help myself and cup her cheek. She feels so soft, a little cold, but very good. "I bought some stuff. Don't ask me the names because I don't remember what they're called. All I know is that they're cleaning supplies, they did the job, and the place is clean." I did fuck up some of the furniture while cleaning but I can get it replaced.

Is it for sure clean? Probably not. I've never cleaned a day in my life. I've always had someone do it for me, but now with Anna, I can't have her do that for me. It seems inappropriate and wrong.

"Sylas." She looks like she's having an internal battle, between panic and disbelief. I'm not sure why and I don't understand why it's so difficult for her to accept my help.

"Anna." I slip my other hand around her back, tugging her closer to me.

"I-I don't know what to say."

"There's nothing you need to say. Just accept this new norm. Stop feeling guilty because I don't and—"

"But what'll happen when you resume hockey? What'll happen if your parents stop by and ask why I'm not cleaning? What do I do when I'm not cleaning?"

"I'll manage. Let me handle it all, and stop worrying. Come over and hang out, and if I'm away, still come over. You like to cook and bake, so use my kitchen. Or, I don't know...take some time for yourself. When Thea is overstimulated, she likes to be alone. If you need that, still come over. You won't need to come through the way you usually do. I've already given them your name downstairs. Just have your ID with you."

There's a mystified look on her face. "You gave them my name? Why?"

"Because you're my girlfriend." God, I love that so fucking much.

"Pretend Sylas, this is pretend." She says *that* word twice as if I need the reminder. I know it is but pretending is also pretending we're not faking it.

"I know, Anna. *I know*," I try to rein the bubbling annoyance at the unnecessary reminder. "But you're still *my* girlfriend. And it would be weird if you weren't on the list. My parents would suspect something. *Please* just..." I wish I could imbed myself in her brain and replace the stubbornness with willingness to accept us. "Go with it. Let yourself let me do things for you. Please."

She appears bashful, hesitant and I almost believe she'll find a way to not agree but she nods. "Okay."

I delicately rub her cheek, reveling in how soft it is and how her pupils expand.

"What's it like?"

Her question confuses me. "What's what like?"

"How easy everything is."

My life in almost every aspect has been easy. It'd be shitty to say it's not. But there are moments when sometimes I wonder if easy is worth it when so much is at stake. The way Mom and Dad could easily take everything away and not bat and eye, especially Dad. He hasn't voiced it directly, but he'll often make off-handed comments about me being *blacklisted* if I don't do as he says.

I don't doubt he'd make it happen, but I also know he wants me to play. Either way, I don't want to find out. All I want is to play hockey. Not have to marry Florence. And see where this *pretend* thing with Anna leads to.

What would she think of me if I told her it's not always easy? Would that make me sound like a piece of shit, considering her situation? Maybe I shouldn't say anything. I'll still sound like one because easy or not, she's having to work, and I'm not. For fuck's sake, I'm paying her to date me because she needs the money that bad.

"I don't know," I answer, unsure. "Never thought about it."

She chuckles and her eyes flutter as my palm drifts down to the side of her neck. "I'm jealous."

"Don't be." I graze my thumb down the column of her neck, feeling it bob. "But I can make things easy for you, if you let me and stop being so stubborn."

"I'm not stubborn." She pouts.

I grin. "Sounds like something a stubborn person would say."

Amusement veils her face.

"Just let me do this for you. Trust me."

Uncertainty flashes in her eyes. "It's crazy..."

"What is?" My gaze drops to her lips.

"This. Us. How it all...just...happened." Her voice is low, husky.

"Do you regret it?" Now my voice is low. Fuck.

"No, but it makes me nervous."

I can't stop staring at her lips. "Do I make you nervous?"

"No...yes. Not in a bad way though," she follows up with a coy smile on her face.

"You'd tell me if something I do makes you uncomfortable?"

She nods. "You make me feel a lot of things. Uncomfortable isn't one of them."

I lean forward, my lips hovering over hers. "What do I make you feel?"

Anna lets out a shaky breath and clutches my arm, the one on her neck. It's warm and the pulse beneath her jaw is thundering. It quickens, faster than before, and her chest expands, brushing against me.

She stands on the tips of her toes, her glossy lips caressing mine. "Hot..."

"Yeah?" I nip her bottom lip.

"Mm-hmm." Her eyes grow heavy, lips pressing against mine.

"I'm chewing gum," I rasp against her mouth as I lift her up. She snakes her legs around my waist and her arms around my neck.

"How is it?"

"Minty." I turn, heading toward the living room.

Anna laughs, making me laugh too, but we stop when I drop down on the sectional. The humor fades when she lands on top of my semi-hard dick, and I tip my head back, clenching my jaw as she begins to grind.

We lock eyes, the silence stretching as the pressure between us thickens. Hers grow heavy, heady, dark, and my dick hardens, throbbing beneath her.

"You're the first person I've ever brought here," I blurt out.

She lifts a brow. "Is that supposed to make me feel special? And I'm pretty certain I saw your teammate here the other day."

That sounded stupid. Why didn't I think it through? I struggle to get my thoughts straight. Looking at her, feeling her, smelling her is too much, but I can't get enough.

"Yes." I tighten my hold on her hips, slowly driving her

against my erection. "And that's not what I meant." I don't bring girls over because it's too intimate, misleading.

"Then what did you mean?" she presses, drawing her hands back to hold mine in place.

"I've never wanted anyone here like this." My gaze trails down the length of her body, stopping where she's sitting on me. "Not until you."

"Wow," she starts, her tone condescending. "I feel so..." With her hands still on mine, I move my palms to her ass and push her against me. Her chest is flush against mine, and her panting breaths fan my face. Her eyes glaze over as her teeth sink into her plump bottom lip, her fingers curling and digging into my shoulders. "Special," she moans quietly.

Anna tightens her grip on my hands, pushing them down and up on her ass.

She lets out a ragged, frustrated breath when I stop moving my hands. I level my gaze with hers, and I get lost in her rich whiskey eyes. *"Você é tão especial para mim. Eu não sei como explicar isso para você. Ou como dizer que eu gosto de você porque eu nunca sentir isso antes."*

A line forms between her brows, eyes narrowing, and a tentative smile curls on her face. "What did you say?"

"What do you think I said?" I move her hands to my shoulders and rest mine on her hips, squeezing once before drifting them south.

She hesitates, her smile turning cunning. "Probably something perverted."

There's no way she understood me. She couldn't have. I spoke too fast.

"Like..." I lean forward, running the tip of my nose along her jaw, down to the side of her neck, inhaling deeply.

She hums and tilts her head to the side, granting me access to her neck as I rub and squeeze her ass. She drags her palm along my short hair, stopping when I nip her skin. The first time is tender, but the second time, I bite with a little more force. Her nails scratch my scalp, and she squirms above me, moaning.

"Like?" I ask again, smirking against the spot I just bit. "Tell me, Anna, what do you think I said?"

"That you're finally going to let me come." She rolls her hips forward and stops scratching. "Because I've been so good and I deserve it."

I look back at her, begging my heart to slow down. "But do you?"

Her eyes turn molten, dark and threatening. "Stop messing with me."

"But *messing* with you is fun," I tease, pressing her against my throbbing cock. I clench my jaw, groaning at the pressure of her pussy. "You're so easy to mess with, play with, do whatever I want with."

It's patronizing, *demeaning* how I hold her against me, how I look at her with every inch of arrogance in me, how I say those words and mean them too.

Anna's jaw hardens and she rolls her lips together before she traps the bottom one between her teeth. Despite how insulted and angry she looks, I can tell she likes this. She squeezes her thighs, sits up straighter, and slackens her arms around my neck.

"And you know it too. The minute I suggested I use your body for money, you should've slapped the shit out of me," I whisper against her ear before I suck the lobe between my teeth, ignoring her protest that her earring is in my mouth. It's comical she's more concerned about them. I draw back a little, rolling her hips again and forcing her to stay still against me. She moans and doesn't push me again, but she does clench her thighs. "Instead, you did as I said and sucked my cock like the good little fuck toy you are. Because that's what you want, right? To be used and degraded. I bet everything in my bank account you're soaking wet. That's how easy *you* are."

Her head dips like she's embarrassed, but I tuck a finger under her chin, forcing her to look at me. "Got nothing to say now?

What happened to that smartass mouth? Where did the Anna go who told me to fuck off?"

I let go of her chin and hip and undo the only two buttons on her collared shirt, untucking it from the waistband of her joggers.

"I need the money," she supplies breathlessly, but her gaze holds challenge, determination. "I'm only here for that."

I stop playing with the hem of her shirt and lean back. "Get off."

Her brows pull in, eyes narrowed as she stares at me, puzzled. But she doesn't climb off me. "What—"

I grab her and gently remove her, setting her on the cushion. Fishing out my phone, I go to my bank account and send her five grand.

"I've sent you money. You should be good for this week. I'll send you more later. You can leave or stay." I straighten, watch the confused expression on her face deepen, and head to my bedroom to grab a tie from my closet.

Not a moment later, she's stepping into my room.

"Sy—"

"Stop," I order before she takes another step away from the door.

"What are you on? Why are you being so—"

"Get on your knees."

She scoffs a laugh. "What?"

"On your knees," I repeat, perching on the edge of my bed.

Her lips part then close as she drops to her knees. "Stop being weird and—"

"On your hands too." My voice is thicker than before, my cock pulsing in my briefs, and despite how badly I want to fix myself, I don't. "Do it, or get out."

She drags her tongue along the top of her teeth, breathes out harshly through her nose before doing as she's told.

The corner of my mouth jerks up, and her eyes catch the movement. It's a smug-as-fuck smile and I don't bother to hold it back this time. Not when she's on her hands and knees for me, staring up at me with disdain. But the heat in her eyes is too hot to ignore, too intense. She could lie, but I know she wants this.

"You're not here because you need the money. You know I'll give it to you. You're here because you want to be treated like a fuck toy. You want to get played with and used. So you're going to crawl to me." I pause and watch her eyes go round, cheeks reddening with realization. "You're going to do it because you want—no, *need* me to use your body however I please. You like to be treated like this. You're here, you're in my room, on your hands and knees, panties dripping wet, *desperate* to be touched. So crawl to me, Anna. Do it now and I'll give you what you really want."

She's wearing the same expression she wore when she had my dick in her mouth. She's intrigued, excited, when she lifts a hand and knee forward. She crawls to me, tentative at first, cheeks red, eyes darting everywhere but at me because I know she's shy about this. Humiliated and in disbelief that she gets off on it.

I can't rip my eyes off her hips and her heart-shaped ass. How it, as well as her breasts, sway with every movement.

When she's at my feet, I grab her arm, and she gasps as I pull her up to stand. "So bloody easy. I can't wait to taste you."

22

ANNA

I KNEW SYLAS WAS BAITING ME. I KNEW WHAT WOULD happen if I followed him upstairs. I knew and I did it anyway because I want this.

I have no idea what'll happen or how, but I don't care because, and as embarrassing as it is, it feels thrilling.

Getting on my knees and crawling? Never in a million years would I have ever thought to do this for anyone, especially for a man. And despite how humiliating it felt, I can't deny the rush that shot through my body.

It was invigorating and intoxicating. What I felt at Salt and when he came to my apartment is exactly how I feel now but a million degrees hotter.

"I knew you'd come," he says, cupping the back of my neck and wrapping the other arm around my back, sealing the space between our lips.

There's nothing soft about the way he kisses me or how he shoves his tongue inside my mouth. It's intense, dizzying, and hard to keep up with. His tongue touches every inch of my mouth, his teeth clash against mine, and my jaw aches from the way he gives as much as he takes.

He forces me on my tiptoes, removes his hand off my neck to grab my ponytail, then yanks hard enough to tip my head back. My scalp screams, but the pulse between my thighs heightens.

I stop breathing when I feel something slip between our mouths, only releasing it when I realize it's his gum. He transferred it seamlessly, despite how frenziedly he kisses me, but once he knows I have it, he pulls back. Still, he keeps a strong grip on my hair, with me on my tiptoes.

"Hold my gum for me," he husks condescendingly. First crawling and now his gum? I can't believe I'm enjoying this. "How is it?"

"Minty," I say, parroting his answer from before.

"How do you feel about being tied up?"

I've never been this hot. I think I might actually be sweating. "Never been tied up before."

"I didn't ask if you have. I said how do you feel about it?" He lifts a brow.

My calves burn, but he doesn't ease his hold on me. "Like I want to try."

He smiles sweetly, too sweetly, and something about it sends an anticipatory shiver down my spine. "Good answer." He releases my hair and waist, letting me stand flat on my feet, then spins us around and pushes me back on the bed.

I fall on my back with a soft bounce. Pushing up on my elbows, I chew his gum as he climbs on the bed, crawls between my thighs, and looms over me.

Time feels like it stops. This feels like more than just pretending, more than just having a good time.

His words from a few minutes ago keep repeating in my head, and I can't get them out. I want to overanalyze them, to demand he translate them, but I don't.

Leaning down, he brushes his lips against mine. His cool minty breath fans them, and I breathe him in. His gaze casts down to our lips and then my chest as it rises and falls a little too haphazardly.

"Are you going to let me have you like you're mine?" He gently nips my top lip. "Use you like you're mine?" Now the bottom. "Lick you like you're mine? Fuck you like you're mine?" He sucks it between his teeth before he releases it and drags his tongue along it.

My eyes flutter closed. "I'm all yours." My voice is a thick rasp, and my breaths become stiff as he pushes up and away from me.

"And don't ever forget that." Sylas flashes me a sly lopsided smile as he lifts my shirt over my breasts. "Fuck, you're so beautiful." He shoves me down so that I'm flat on my back, darting his tongue from my sternum, down to my stomach, past my belly button, to the waistband of my joggers.

I muffle my moan, enjoying how his warm tongue feels on my skin. He slides off my pants, removes my shoes, and tosses them both somewhere.

"Sit up," he orders, and when I do, he removes my shirt and bra. I'm sitting on the edge of his bed in nothing but my thong and socks. "Goddamn, Anna."

"Stop looking and touch me, please," I plead, lying back and spread my thighs for him, not feeling the slightest bit embarrassed by how wet the dark red fabric between my legs is.

"Arms up." He grabs a tie I hadn't realized was on his bed and wraps it tightly around my wrists.

"What purpose does this serve?" I ask when he lifts my arms over my head.

"There really isn't one." He opens the drawer of his nightstand and rifles around inside.

"Then why did you—"

He drops to his knees on the floor, grabs my thighs, and throws my legs over his shoulders. "It's knowing that I have so much control over you, and that you'll let me do what I want and not ask questions. Now make sure you keep your arms up or I'll stop."

Wow.

I nod heedlessly, breathing in a shaky breath when his head dips and I feel his tongue over the drenched cotton. Air leaves me when he laps over me, and my eyes roll back when he drags his tongue up and down.

"Oh—" I moan, almost tempted to drop my hands, but fist them instead. "Mo...more." I chew on the gum, slow, grinding it between my teeth.

Sylas's fingers dig into my thighs, squeezing them hard. I'm sure his blunt nails will leave indentations, maybe even bruises from how hard he's holding me, but I don't care. I push into him, back arching, as more breathless moans slip past my lips.

But when he stops, I almost scream from the intense pressure spreading. My hands twitch, fingers digging into my palms, reminding myself not to drop my arms.

He slides my thong down my thighs, the slick material leaving a wet path, and continues past my knees and ankles. As he does, he licks my arousal off my leg, leaving his own trail of saliva.

"God," I whimper impatiently, desperately.

"No. *Sylas*," he corrects, voice coarse and just as desperate as the sounds leaving my mouth. "The only name coming out of your mouth will be the name of the person between your thighs."

"*Yes.*" I exhale a ragged breath.

He throws my thong over his shoulder, placing my thighs back where he had them, his mouth where I want it the most. He doesn't play or taunt me; he licks me long and deep, his tongue right at my entrance. He moans, the vibration of it sending a shiver down my body, but I freeze when he thrusts his tongue inside me. He drives it as far as it'll go, twisting and massaging me in a way that has me questioning my existence. I don't understand how his tongue is doing what it's doing. All I know is that I'm trembling, hips bucking up because I need more pressure, something to ease the tension on my aching clit.

"Sylas, I need more," I beg, gasping, eyes rolling back as his tongue flicks inside me fast and hard. He grunts against me, and I think I hear him swallow and then again as if he were drinking me, holy fuck, *he is*, he's drinking me. Fuck. "Please...m-m-more. More!"

He draws his tongue out of me, and I sag against the bed with a huff. He looms over me again, mouth glistening with my arousal. But when I catch sight of something pink and hear a soft whirring sound, I freeze once more.

Sitting up, I see a mini wand vibrator in his hand.

"Get off," I grit, bringing my palms to his chest and shoving him away.

His worried green eyes sweep over me. "What's wrong? Did I do something—"

"You've got to be kidding me. Who knows who you've used that on. *Never brought anyone here—* Can't believe I fell for that. Get off."

"I'm many things, but a liar isn't one of them. Your jealousy is so fucking hot." Leaving it still on, he drops the toy next to me, brings his hand over his head, and lifts his shirt off. "You're the first person here and you'll be the last."

I'm glaring, but he only smirks. "Sylas, I'm serious."

"I bought this and a few other things earlier today, but we're starting slow." He brings his lips to mine, his voice not playful or taunting like before. "Trust me, Anna. *Trust me*. Please?"

I don't think—no, I know he's not lying. I don't know why I trust him so much, but I do. And my resolve crumbles.

"Okay, I trust you." I lie back down.

His beautiful, sculpted chest and torso are on display for me to see but unfortunately not feel with my wrists tied. If I could, I'd chart a path over every inch of his skin, exploring like I've been wanting to since the other night.

"I'll show you the receipt later. I promise." He grabs the wand and holds it next to my mouth, dragging the round silicone over my lips, and settles his thick thigh between my pussy, pinning my arms over my head. "Open your mouth. Get it nice and wet for me."

My lips part wider, letting him swirl the toy around my tongue until it's sopping wet with my saliva. Then he pulls it out and trails it down my throat, to my hard nipples.

The toy vibrates against me, the rapid motion inviting the pressure between my thighs to deepen. Desperate for relief, I rub myself against his jean-clad thigh.

He holds the toy and his thigh down, and brings his mouth to my other nipple, playing with the piercing. He rolls his tongue around it, lapping and flicking it fast.

"Yes! Yes, just like that!" I cry out as I continue to grind myself against him. I'm drowning in a pleasure so intense I start shaking.

He doesn't let up, but when he bites the mere tip of my nipple and tugs it hard, I come so fiercely my back lifts off the bed.

Even when he removes his mouth and the toy, I'm moaning, not processing what's happening until I see him drop to his knees again and hitch my thighs over his shoulders.

"Say *bells* and I'll stop." His voice is so gruff, so deep, it doesn't sound like him. "Okay? You'll say it, right?"

"Okay, I'll say it." I clutch at the comforter as he idly drags the toy along my inner thigh.

My body jerks, restless with anticipation. I hold my breath, stop moving when I feel the vibrations on my pussy lips, and when his hungry, heated eyes level with mine, a proud smile curls on his face.

He doesn't have to say what he's thinking, I can feel it. Neither does he have to say anything degrading because he knows I'm on the edge. He knows he could ask me to do just about anything and I would. He looks smug as fuck because he knows if he asked, I'd get on my knees for him, and I'd beg for it too.

Spreading my thighs wider for him, I resume chewing on the gum, my nostrils flaring. "Unless you say *bells*, I won't stop."

With no warning, he spreads my lips, baring my throbbing clit to him, and lays the pulsating toy on it. My eyes roll back, my jaw goes slack, and I fist the bed for support before I levitate off. Then he once again thrusts his tongue into my entrance.

There is so much going on, I can't focus on one particular thing other than making sure I don't drop my hands. My thighs are quivering, and my heart is thundering so fast, I'm afraid it'll jump out of my rib cage.

"Sylas, yes! Fuck, don't stop." I'm whimpering, clenching my teeth from the intensity of the way he moves his tongue, swallows my arousal, and swirls the round silicone around my clit. "Fuu-uck. Fuuck, Sy-Sy-Sylas...Oh!" I crane my neck back, muscles coiled tight.

I come again, screaming his name as he plays with me. He doesn't let up on the toy or his tongue, and I'm certain he raised the vibration level because it whirs louder, faster.

He holds it down firmly, slipping his tongue out, and licks my pussy, giving it deep attention. I'm spasming and crying, squeezing my eyes tight as the pressure at the pit of my stomach builds again. But a second later it explodes and I'm coming harder than before, my jaw aching from how wide it's parted.

I'm breathing harshly, and despite *bells* clinging to the tip of my tongue, I don't say it. Not when he drops my shaky legs, grabs my hips, and flips me on my stomach.

"Get on your knees," he instructs gruffly, and I do. Slowly, but I do.

My chest is pressed against his bed, nipples scraping against the comforter and ass in the air. I don't get to question what he'll do because he slaps my ass cheeks so hard I feel each ripple, each sting, and the gratification grips my every nerve with a sweltering heat.

I release a long string of curse words in groans, stopping only when he slips the toy between my thighs and makes sure it's buried between my pussy lips.

"Squeeze your thighs around it and don't drop it." He slaps my ass harder than before, and because of it, I clench my thighs.

"Fuck," I breathe, biting the comforter and making a mess

with my drool. It grazes my clit, my suspicions cementing—he *definitely* upped the level again. It feels…oh God, this feels insane, I'm coming again. How is that possible? "Sy…Sy…" I can't get his full name out of my mouth.

A mix between a moan, a cry, and choppy breaths are the only sounds leaving my mouth. I'm not sure I'm making all three because I'm spasming out. My brain is in a deep fog, and I can't articulate a thought or word. I'm not sure I'm breathing anymore.

"You're unbelievable. So hot, I can't get over you…over your ass," he praises, rubbing my ass cheek with his rough palm before he removes the toy. He throws it on the bed next to my face, and I catch the glistening rubber before I close my eyes. Then I hear his zipper and the rustle of his jeans and shoes coming off.

"Mmm…" is all I can muster, still reeling from the orgasms. Every few seconds, I shudder, my clit pulsing and my thighs clenching as if my body were still chasing the high.

"More?" he roughs out, his long fingers gliding down my burning cheek between my thighs and over my soaking wet folds.

"More." I sigh contentedly, nodding despite my brain telling me it's enough. I know what's coming and I want to feel him everywhere.

He drives a finger inside me fast, palm slapping over me hard. My breath gets caught, and I sink my face into the bed, biting the comforter as he fucks me with a finger, but when he adds another, I quickly contract around them. He's moving them in a way that feels unreal, deep. I feel his knuckle graze me, feel his fingers curve and scissor inside me. They hit a spot so sensitive I'm squealing and rocking my ass into his hand because I can't get enough. I can't stop chasing the orgasm, can't stop begging for it.

"Just like that! Sylas, yes! Just…" I scream as he continues to use his fingers to squeeze the orgasm out of me. "…like that."

I'm slowly rocking as I come down from it and inhaling deeply when I feel him remove his fingers. I focus on nothing but getting my breathing under control.

I hear the faint ripping sound and when I open my eyes, I see the condom foil flailing in the air until it lands on the bed.

"Ready?" The tip of his cock nudges my entrance.

No. Of course I'm not. I've seen his dick. I've had it in my mouth. I know how thick and large he is, bigger than anything I've ever had. It's insane, really. Regardless, I find myself nodding and saying, "Yes."

"Such a good toy." He slides his length between my lips, hitting my clit with every stroke until I'm squirming and moving my ass closer to him. "So easy to use."

I clench my core at his words alone. "Please," I whimper, arching my back like a cat and further spreading myself for him.

I'm stuck in a daze, high up in the clouds, relentless, eager, and so turned on. "Do it," I plead.

And he does. He slowly sinks his tip into me, the stretch beyond magnificent. "Holy shit." I grind my teeth and he groans, one hand squeezing my hip, the other I assume on his shaft, guiding himself inside me.

"Anna, fuuuck, fuuuck..." His fingers dig, squeeze, and pinch my skin as he slips in a little deeper. With every push, I find myself clenching around him, holding my breath because despite him being in my mouth, this is different. He's so thick, I feel like I'm on the verge of losing my goddamn mind. "Anna, *meu bem*, relax, breathe, you're so fucking tight. I *need* you to relax." I think he folds in on himself because I feel his warm, sweaty chest against my back, lips on my shoulder, teeth biting my skin. I wouldn't be surprised if his teeth marks are there tomorrow. "I *fucking* need you to relax. I'm losing my mind over you. Fucking hell Anna... fuuuck."

I can't say anything but make myself pliable to him as he thrusts deeper inside. Everything feels hazy, slow, and so out of my control. I'm gripping on to the comforter, biting it too.

But it's not until he plunges all the way inside that I feel every inch of him. His balls slap my clit, and both his hands hug my hips. The loud slap, the slick sound of our sweaty skin, and our voices all echo throughout the room. He stills against me, gritting his teeth.

"You're unreal." I hear the awe in his voice and then feel him pull out slightly before he's ramming back against me. "I don't think I'll ever be able to get over this." And he repeats the motion. "Over you."

I cry out, eyes rolling back when he does it again and again until my pussy adjusts to the size of him. "Har-harder. Go harder. Fuck me faster."

He chuckles roughly and rocks his hips forward, his cock deeper than ever. It hits a spot I didn't think was possible. His balls slap against my clit, the noises so lewd, so fucking filthy, I'm getting wetter at the sound of them.

He works fast, hard, just like I begged for, but the intensity of the way he fucks makes me almost beg him to stop. I'm jerking with every thrust, my nipples sensitive from how they rub against the comforter. Another orgasm is building up. I'm so close I can feel it. Any second now, I'm going to come, but his words freeze the desire to do so.

"Don't you dare come until I do. You're going to come with me," he demands. I hear how hard his teeth scrape against each other, and how his breathing is harsh and out of control. His movements are the same too, shaky and desperate.

I bite my lip, holding back from coming, but when I peer over my shoulder, I see him staring at my ass. It bounces and ripples, and I feel him spread my cheeks and stare at my asshole. When his eyes collide with mine, he flashes me the most wicked smirk and spits between my cheeks before raising his hand and spreading his saliva.

That's so hot. Why is that so hot? Holy fuck.

He doesn't push his finger in even though my asshole is strangely twitching like it wants him to. I think I want him to, too. He only rubs around and over it but stops abruptly and drops his head back, the veins on his neck popping. His movements turn sloppy and he grunts, "Come now."

That's all it takes because, on command, everything I was holding in bursts and I'm coming undone right underneath him.

I'm not sure how I'll ever recover, and I continue this line of thinking as he eventually pulls out of me. I hate how empty I feel, and if my energy levels weren't so depleted, I'd ask him to fuck me again.

I can't get my breathing under control. I can't do anything but think about what life will be like moving forward.

Nothing will ever compare. No other person and certainly not any toy. I'm so fucked.

Flopping flat on my stomach, I stay still and pry one eye open when Sylas lies next to me and sets a small piece of white paper down.

"What's that?" I ask hoarsely, taking in his flushed face, his sweaty, nude body, and his muscles bulging as he slips off the tie.

"The receipt," he pants out.

I smile lazily, my eyes barely staying open. "You didn't have to show it to me. I trust you."

"I did. I bought a ball gag. Need to know how you feel about those." Sylas returns a dazed smile of his own. "Oh, and give me my gum back." He cups the back of my head, gently pulls me in, and kisses me softly. He slips his tongue inside my mouth, stroking my tongue until he feels the gum and takes it back into his mouth.

Wow, that was—wait, did he say ball gag?

23

SYLAS

"Cig me." Marc cups his palms, holding them up.

"Yeah, here." I pat my pocket until I find what I'm looking for, fish it out, and throw it to him as we walk out of the rink.

"What the hell is this?" He holds up the stick of gum, waving it in the air. "I need—"

"I don't do that anymore." I blow out a breath, a white puffy cloud billowing in front of me before it disappears.

He freezes mid-step, staring at me, dumbfounded. I keep walking, knowing he'll follow behind me, and he does a moment later.

"Since when?" I don't look at him, but I know his eyes are trained on me. "Stop fucking with me."

"I'm not." I shove my cold hands in my pockets. "Anna doesn't like it and—"

He bursts out laughing. "Holy shit."

"Let's not do this. We're dating and—"

"It's fake, Sylas. Remember? You guys are faking this because of your dad and mom and...and...oh...*oh*." Realization deepens his voice.

I stop walking, pivot, and wait for him to get it out. Huffing out a breath, I pull my phone out and check the time, making sure I have enough time for this conversation. Anna and I made plans to meet after practice, and although we didn't settle on a time, I don't want to keep her waiting.

"Well?" I stare at him expectantly because he has yet to say a word. Instead, he's staring at me like I'm a damn fish out of water. "Marc? Stop looking at me like that. Just say what you need to say."

He wipes his palms down his face, chuckling in disbelief. "I'm just...shocked. Like...really...just...shocked."

I impatiently stare at him. "Yes, you already said that. You have anything else to say? If not, I need to go."

Marc grins widely. "I don't know whether to congratulate you or offer my condolences."

That confuses me. "Why?"

"Because this isn't just a crush. You're absolutely down bad for this girl. This is either going to be the best or the worst thing to ever happen to you." He muses. "You and cigarettes are like the devil, and hell, you can't picture one without the other. Did you just up and quit?"

I nod, indifferent. "It's not a big deal."

"Did she tell you to stop, or did you do it by choice?"

"It was my choice."

"Christ." He snuffs a chuckle, running his palms over his beanie. "Wait, did you sleep with her? Is that why—"

"No." I shift my weight from one foot to the other. "I mean, we have, but it's not like that." I drag my fingers through my hair, grazing the tips of my cold ears. "Don't be a dick."

My heart picks up, my chest rises a little faster, and my palms sweat.

"I'm not," he scoffs, raising his hands in surrender. "I'm never a dick unless necessary. You know that."

"I'm serious. I'm going to tell you something and I don't

want you messing with me because it's freaking me out," I warn him.

He smiles like the asshole that he is, but then he softens. "I promise I won't."

"I like seeing her every day, and I'm not saying that because I expect or want sex. We wouldn't need to do anything because I look forward to just *seeing* her."

If he looks shocked now, I can't imagine how he'd react if he knew how heavy my heart is beating, how my palms are profusely sweating, how my body feels ready to bolt to be with her, how my brain keeps replaying her smile and the sound of her raspy laugh.

"Damn." He draws out the word. "You're in deep." He stands there, unblinking. Despite what he said, he doesn't sound like he's processing it. "So...*deep.*"

"Yeah, I am. I can't believe I'm saying this, but I really like her. I woke up thinking about her and haven't been able to stop," I say, wiping my palms on my hips. Marc detects the motion but doesn't call me out on it. "I'm so into her, but I don't know what she feels for me. I don't want to ask because I don't want to make things weird or make her feel like she needs to tell me what I want to hear because of our arrangement."

He clicks his tongue, eyes incredulous and mouth dropped so low, it could touch the concrete. "Jesus, Sylas."

"I know." It's freezing as shit out here, but I can't stop sweating.

"This has nothing to do with me, but it's still stressing me out. I really need a cigarette." He removes his beanie and drags his fingers through his black hair.

"You have gum. Use it." I grab two pieces, remove the foil, and pop them in my mouth. Gum will never be the same; I can't even chew it anymore without thinking of her. "I don't know what to do."

Marc accepts he's not going to get a cigarette and slips the stick into his mouth. "This is shit." He chews aggressively.

"I know. The cubes are better, but this is easier to carry."

He's quiet for a long moment, making me feel uneasy, but then he blows a bubble and stifles a laugh. "Get your shit together. You're never like this. Just talk to her. If you have feelings, I'm sure she's developed them too."

I attempt to conjure every ounce of nonchalance from within. "I don't know. She doesn't do boyfriends."

"But she's sure doing you," he replies simply, giving me a pointed stare.

I huff. "That's different."

"It's not. Talk to her. You've never been afraid to say how it is. Don't start now."

"I know…"

I'm a confident person, but right now, I'm nervous. I shouldn't be, and it's stupid to feel like this, but it's the effect she has on me.

It's strange how one girl can make everything—*correction*: make *me* crumble.

"You sure know how to complicate things." He doesn't bother to hold back his laughter this time. "Don't stress. I'm certain she's into you as much as you're into her."

I'm hoping he's right.

I meet Anna at the Columbus Circle holiday market.

She looks casual but pretty, wearing a cream-colored puffer jacket, a red-and-white-striped scarf, and light denim jeans that hug her hips and thighs. She's wearing glasses and her hair is wavy instead of its usual straight style.

I aim for calm and cool when I stop in front of her, but her lips curl into a smile that's now engraved in my head, and then I get a hint of perfume: apples, cinnamon, and maple. It smells good. I discreetly inhale and do it again because I can't get enough of it or her.

It must cloud my thoughts because before I know it, I'm blurting, "You look really pretty and you smell good too."

Her cheeks, already slightly pink from the chill that nips at them, are a shade darker. She brushes her bangs away, grinning sheepishly. "Thanks. You think I look festive enough?"

I slowly take her in again, absorbing every inch of her. My heart patters rapidly and my palms sweat again. "Super festive. I like your earrings." I glance at the red bells that hang from her bow earrings and the other tiny hoops and studs that decorate her ear. "Do you have an earring for every day, or what?" I tease.

She touches them. "And holiday. I feel naked if I don't wear them."

I grin, making a mental note of that. "Ready to check out the booths?"

She's not cleaning for me anymore, and after I told her I'd never been to a holiday market, she demanded we come to one. It wouldn't take much convincing on her part because I'd do whatever she asked.

After all, she's my girlfriend. It's my job to take her out on dates. Do what she wants, when she wants.

"How have you been living in New York for as long as you have and never been to one?" she asks as we stroll into the market side by side.

"My parents, especially Mom, have never cared for them. I'm sure you can imagine what she thinks of them." I tuck my hands in my pockets, not because I'm cold but because they won't stop sweating. I can't believe this is what a crush feels like. "And I guess living here for so long, I've become jaded to it all. If I wasn't in school or training, I was in Colorado snowboarding or in the tropics or something." I'm not trying to brag, but it's just what I did, and I wanted to be away from all the bright lights and decor.

"Or something?" she asks, poking my side. She didn't make a comment about my parents, but I'm sure she's thinking about it.

"Fiji, the Maldives, Mexico…" I trail off. I could list all the places my parents have taken Thea and me, but I don't want to make this about me. "How's your arm, by the way?"

"Just a little sore." Her gaze flicks to her covered arm then back at me. In spite of the frosty weather, the way she looks at me makes my body blister. "How's yours?"

"Sore, very sore."

She pins me with a disbelieving look. "You don't feel it anymore, do you?"

I hold back my smile. "No, I don't but I think everything I drank played a role in that."

Anna scoffs. "We drank just about the same."

"But I'm also taller and weigh over two hundred pounds," I point out.

"Is it that or because you get hit so much on the ice, you hardly feel it now?" she says as we stop in front of a booth that sells candles. She picks up one on display, inhales it, then holds it up for me to smell. I shake my head at the peppermint scent, and she scrunches her nose in agreement. "But I suppose the gear is there to protect you. So even with all of it on, does it hurt when you get struck with a puck?"

She picks up another, inhales it, then does a double take on the label, smelling it again. Meanwhile, I'm still stuck on what she said. I love that she looked me up and watched my games.

A megawatt smile spreads across my face. "Yeah, it hurts, especially if it gets you where the gear doesn't cover."

I grab her hand, lifting the candle to my nose. I take a whiff and then another but a long one, my lungs filling up with whatever the scent is. It smells like whatever Anna has on, and I glance at the label. *'TIS THE SEASON* it's called.

"Smells good." I tentatively let go of her hand, grabbing two brand-new candles from the shelf. Never cared for candles, but I guess I'll make this one the exception.

"It—what are you doing?" Her gaze flicks to them as she places the other back.

"I'm buying them."

"Why?"

"Because you like it. I like it. And when you like something, you buy it."

She doesn't look as amused as I do. "You don't have to be a smartass. You don't—"

I lean down, my lips over her ear, hand clutching her waist. I make it quick because the sales lady stalls just a few feet away, watching us. "Don't play the 'poor, woe is me, don't buy me that because I'm an independent woman' bullshit. I'm not trying to be a pretentious, shallow asshole, but if I have to, I will. I'm buying it because I have the money, so don't be a brat and just accept it. And remember, I'm your boyfriend. If I want to spoil my girl-friend, I will."

I squeeze her gently once before I let her go.

She rolls her eyes but I can see the way her lips subtly jerk up. "I am an independent woman, and I do know how to accept things. I just don't usually have someone wanting to buy me things. But whatever, it's your money and just so you know, one candle is forty dollars."

"And this jacket was three grand, so what's your point?" I toss out.

"Do you even like candles?"

She picks up another, sniffs it, then holds it up to my nose.

"No, but I like this one." I shrug. It's okay, but I don't think I'll like another as much as the one that reminds me of her.

She grins, putting it back and picks up a few more that we smell. Once we're done and I go to pay, she doesn't fight me.

"This better not be some charity thing. I swear if there's a camera crew following me, I'll kill you," she threatens when we step out of the booth, jabbing a finger at my chest.

"Don't worry, I already ticked off doing charity this year. Remember the auction?" I say, getting a glare and middle finger from her. I laugh, hooking my cold one around hers. "That's not very nice of you. You do that again and you'll end up on the naughty list."

"Find me there next to you." Her cheek twitches, and she squeezes my finger.

"Next to you?" I hum, doing a long and slow perusal of her body. "I'm fine with that."

Something sparks in her eyes, and I wonder, *pathetically*, if she feels what I feel. I desperately want her to.

"Well, come on, we have three hours and many more booths to go." Anna drops our hands but doesn't let go of my finger. She tugs me along while I hold the pale red paper bag holding our candles, and I follow like a dog.

24

ANNA

Saturday, December 21

"I CAN'T BELIEVE I LEAVE AND THIS HAPPENS." JENNY shakes her head in, staring at me with a shell-shocked expression from the screen of my phone. "I'm going to need you to start from the beginning, and don't leave a single detail out."

I drop onto the plush bench in the fitting room and exhale a fatigued breath. I came to get a dress for Sylas's parents' Christmas party. We were supposed to go yesterday, but after the holiday market, we went to see the Rockefeller Christmas tree, then skated a little. By the time we were done, we were cold, so we went back to his penthouse. One moment I was sitting on his kitchen island and then we were getting undressed, every inch of him all over me.

We agreed to go today but his dad called and said he needed to practice. Sylas said as much as he wished he could've told him no, hockey is the one thing his dad won't take no for an answer.

I told him I'd be okay doing this alone. Although after coming to a few stores he recommended, I wish he was here. I felt out of place at some of the stores Sylas recommended, and while most of the sales associates are nice, some of them are definitely judging me.

Thankfully I've already found a dress, so I won't need to keep shopping. But now that I'm done, I wish Sylas were here. I've gotten used to his presence. It's strange when I don't see him or talk to him. I haven't since nine this morning and it's already six.

"Jenny, I've already told you everything *and* in detail."

She's still not back and probably won't be until the break is over. Though we've been talking and I've shared Sylas's proposal to fake dating, sex, the money, everything. She was shocked then and still is, not that I blame her. I'm still not over how everything has played out.

"I know. I'm—it's just—I can't believe that you two—I'm sorry." She chuckles, her face the image of bewilderment. "It's insane."

"Trust me, I know. I still can't believe this is happening. That we're doing this and how real it feels." I stare at myself in the fitting room's full-length mirror, eyeing the hickeys on my breasts and hips.

She gasps, wide eyes sparkling. "Is this you finally admitting what you've been in denial about?"

I set the phone down and grab my shirt, pulling it over my head. Since telling her, she's been asking the same question I've been avoiding.

"Yeah, I like him. I like him a lot." I shakily breathe, attempting to get the crazy flutters that burst in my stomach under control.

I didn't want to believe I did. I thought maybe it was just infatuation, something that would pass, but it's not. Night and day, I'm thinking about him. I count down the seconds to see him, absorb the sound of his voice, revel in the feel of his rough hands on my skin. And I don't mean that in a purely sexual way. I just like how he touches me with care, like I'm special to him.

I guess I am, since I'm his pretend girlfriend. But I wish I weren't; I wish I could take *pretend* out of the sentence.

She buries her face into her pillow, muffling her squeal. Lifting her head, she has a shit-eating grin on her face. "I can't believe my Anna has feelings for someone."

"Shut up." I smile awkwardly as I grab my jeans. "It's embarrassing to feel this way."

Jenny laughs, sitting up against the headboard. "No, it's cute."

"Cute? Or delusional?" I button my jeans and slip my boots on. "It's not real. Everything we're doing is fake and—"

"Let's not do this."

"Not do what?" I grab my jacket off the hook, along with my purse and the dress I'll be buying.

"Act like something isn't there. You're too smart to act stupid. It's obvious he likes you, and don't say it's because of his parents. I'm sure to some degree it is and while I won't pretend to know him, I don't think he'd go out of his way to do this for the hell of it."

I know she's right, but I'm a little afraid to believe there's more and then have it blow up in my face. There's this feeling in my stomach, warning me to be careful, but at the same time, it's telling me to go for it. I've never felt like this and it's freaking me out a little.

I want to go for it because the signs are there. I'd be stupid to act like they're not, stupid to believe he's just being nice or going out of his way because I'm doing him a favor, but it feels more than that.

"Don't overcomplicate it. Go for it," she urges, voice giddy, like she really believes everything will work out between Sylas and me.

And all I can do is hope I'm not setting myself up for failure.

25

SYLAS

STANDING OUTSIDE ANNA'S DOOR, I STARE AT THE crooked brass number on the frame then down at my lopsided bow tie. When I go to fix it, the door swings open and the world around me ceases to exist.

I breathe in but don't exhale, the air getting caught and trapped in my lungs.

Anna is *striking*. I'm in a state of shock, unable to fathom forming a single thought or word to convey just how gorgeous she looks.

"You look..." Her words ebb, eyes trailing down the length of my body and back up, stopping when they reach my neck. She takes a step forward, lifting her hands. "May I?"

"Yeah." I swallow, nodding. My gaze darts to every inch of her, soaking everything in all at once. "I look what?"

My lungs burn, begging for air, and when I take a breath, I'm drowned in the scent of her perfume: apples, cinnamon, maple, reminding me of the candle sitting on my nightstand.

She gently adjusts my bow tie, peering up at me from her

thick black lashes, her dark whiskey eyes boring into mine. When she's done, she doesn't move her fingers. They stay on the rounded edges of the black silk.

I trace over the line of her lips, at the red color that paints them, and I watch fixedly as they move when she talks. "You look very handsome."

That makes me feel good, but it's hard to focus on the words when I can't stop replaying the sound of her soft, seductive voice. Or the way her lips parts to speak, teeth just barely grazing the inside of her bottom lip, her tongue shifting with every syllable.

I smile, settling my gaze on her face. I inhale a slow breath, filling my lungs with her perfume. "And you look…" I close my mouth because I still haven't found an appropriate word for how she looks. "Divine. Mesmerizing."

They're not my best work, but they are the only ones that came to mind. I am, though, mesmerized.

She's wearing a long black dress that hugs her body in a way that's both modest and sexy. The straps purposely hang off her shoulders, there's a small dip in the neckline that exposes just a bit of her cleavage, and the slit on the side of her leg stops mid-thigh, giving me a view of her heels and the thin black straps around her ankles.

Expelling a quiet breath, I force myself to look up at her again.

"Yeah, you are the personification of the word *beautiful*. I'm sorry." I grab a wisp of her bang, twirling the black strand around my finger. I eye the gold earrings and the small studs on her ears, the clear lens that covers the surface of her eye, and the tight slicked-back bun.

Her lips part as they curl upward into a demure smile. "What are you sorry for?"

"That those are the only words I was able to come up with. They don't do you justice."

Her already pink cheeks darken and her eyes glimmer as they

leisurely sweep over my face. "You said I'm the personification of *beautiful*. That's the nicest compliment I've ever received. Nothing will ever top it. You've just set the standard." She drops her hands to her sides. "So, it's safe to say I did good?"

I'm grinning hard, just as she's beaming when I grab her hand and spin her around. "More than good. I can't wait to show you off."

Anna giggles when I wrap an arm around her back and draw her to my chest. "Because I look good?"

"No, because you're mine." My voice deepens, not like it did the other night. It sounds rough and possessive. I should tone it down, but I don't want to. I don't want to fake it anymore, and after tonight, I want to take *pretend* out of our relationship.

"Ready?" I quietly ask as we enter my parents over-the-top Christmas-decorated home. It's not gaudy but it's very in your face.

I'd be lying if I said it's not pretty. I know it is, and I can tell Anna feels the same way as her gaze veers over every decoration in wonderment.

"Yeah."

"If anyone makes you feel uncomfortable, if they're pushy, annoying you, being rude, or invasive...touch your earring or say *bells*, and we'll get the fuck out of here," I tell her, but her lips quirk up, eyes shining.

I gave her a rundown of what things would be like when we came here. The majority of my parents' friends are pretentious, shallow-minded people. Anna said she'd be okay because of her working at the restaurant and cleaning homes, but this is different. These *people* aren't just anybody, they're celebrities—everything from professional athletes, models, actors and actresses, and CEOs. They're not worried about wandering eyes or listening ears because what happens here, stays here.

Not that anything bizarre happens other than the drugs, the alcohol, the men bringing their mistresses, and whatever happens in the tucked-away rooms in my parents' home.

She rubs her thumb over my hand. "I promise to warn you, but don't worry. I'll be okay."

"I know. Everyone here is particular, and I know what they're like."

Anna smiles, easing the discomfort in my chest. "I get it. Everything will be okay."

I can't help myself so I kiss the top of her head, careful not to mess a strand out of place. "Yeah, it will. I'm happy you came."

"Thanks for invit—"

"Oh, hi, Anna dear." Mom cuts her off mid-sentence, snaking her arms around her, catching us off guard. "Just look at you." She keeps her hands on her shoulders and sweeps her gaze over Anna's dress, hair, and makeup. "You look beautiful." She flashes her a prim smile.

"Thank you, and thank you for having me here." She returns a friendly smile of her own.

Mom waves a dismissive hand. "No, don't thank me. You're Sylas's girlfriend. We're so glad you're here."

I hear the tightness in her voice, but it's gone before it settles in the space between us. I don't doubt Anna heard it too, but she's good about keeping her smile pasted on her face.

Surprisingly, my parents haven't asked about Anna or made comments about our relationship. I thought by now they would have. It's hard to believe they're one hundred percent okay with it, considering just a few weeks ago, Mom was desperately trying to make Florence and me happen.

"Sy, sweetheart." Mom directs her attention to me. "Can I speak to you for a moment?"

"I don't want to leave—"

"Don't worry. I won't take you away from her for long." Now she looks at Anna, lips stretched impossibly wide. "Anna will be okay alone for a few minutes. Isn't that right, dear?"

"Uh..." She wavers before she nods. "Yeah, I'll be okay."

I cock a brow, grabbing her hand. Mom tracks the movement, the faintest crease forming between her smooth skin.

Disregarding that, I look at Anna. "Are you sure?"

"I'm sure." She stands on her tiptoes and places a chaste kiss on my cheek, then rubs the spot to clean the lipstick she probably left behind. "Take your time. I'll be here." She squeezes then lets go of my hand.

Mom stands there, watching us keenly, but still I hesitate. "I won't take long."

"I promise I'll make it quick." She ushers me away, but I look over my shoulder at Anna. She gives me a thumbs-up before she disappears from view.

We step into the office where I expect to find Dad, but it's just us.

"Are you sure this is what you want?" she candidly asks.

I breathe in, willing for all the patience in the world. I know what she's asking, but I need to hear her say it. "Sure about what?"

"You and Anna. Sy, she's a beautiful girl, smart too, but she's not Florence."

"And thank God for that. If I wanted Florence, I'd be with Florence, but there is nothing there. I want and like Anna. Please..." I pinch the bridge of my nose, exhaling sharply. "Accept it, but even if you don't, it isn't going to change anything. Anna is my girlfriend and it's going to stay that way."

"I just wanted to make sure. If she's who you want to be with, I'll accept it." She squares her shoulders, her lips thinning in a flat line, the corners of her eyes strained. "As promised, I told you I wouldn't take long. Go be with Anna." She places a stiff palm on my cheek, rubbing her thumb in circles on it. "Will we see you tomorrow morning for the pictures?"

"I'll be here." I smile.

"Good." She drops her hand.

As soon as she guides me outside, I search for Anna. It takes me a little longer to find her because I keep getting stopped and asked questions about hockey, school, and more hockey. When I do find her, she's surrounded by my friends and sister. She's smiling at whatever Frost's just said, then laughing at Berlin.

I immediately stand next to her, wrapping my arm around her waist and tugging her to my side.

Frost smirks at the motion, knowing I'm telling him to fuck off.

"Sorry for taking a while," I say in her ear.

"It's okay. I found Thea and then the guys showed up," she replies.

"Don't worry, Sy. We were keeping her company. She wasn't lonely," Frost chimes in.

I pin him with an irked look, my fingers clutching her hip. "I—"

"No, but I'm glad you're back," Anna supplies, nuzzling closer to me so our bodies are flush.

That slaps away the stupid smirk on Frost's face. It dawns on him, as well as Berlin. Meanwhile, Marc is looking altogether too smug, and I know there's a "told you so" on the tip of his tongue. I'm sure they figured it was fake because they know how pushy Mom has been about Florence. They're smart enough to add two plus two, but I'm sure they didn't expect how naturally we look and act.

But it's not acting, at least not anymore.

"Did he coerce you, Anna? Don't be scared. We're here for you," Berlin teases. "If you need help getting out of this, say the word and we'll help you. Don't feel like you need to deal with this on your own."

I roll my eyes, but Anna laughs. "No, I really like this—Sylas. I like us. I'm all right."

My cheeks warm because she sounds sincere and squeezes my hand as if she were reassuring me.

Marc cocks his head to the side, the expression on his face saying *If that isn't a sign, I don't know what is.*

I nod in return, letting him know it's going to happen.

26

ANNA

Wednesday, 12:00 a.m. December 25

SYLAS HAS BEEN WEIRD SINCE WE ARRIVED BACK AT HIS penthouse.

He was fine all night, laughing, smiling, throwing jokes with his friends, Thea, and anyone he spoke with. Although aside from his friends and sister, I could tell he was—for the most part—playing nice. He didn't tell me, but I could hear the faux enthusiasm in his voice, see the corners of his mouth curl in a tight smile, and notice his stance was slightly rigid anytime he spoke with his father's closest friends about hockey.

I could see the pressure strain his shoulders, like their words were heavy on him. It was bad when his father would show up and force himself into the conversation, adding stress I could visibly see on Sylas.

It was extra, but I'd insert myself in the conversation or ask Sylas for a drink. I could tell the men didn't care for me or like it, but it helped Sylas. He was back to being himself, arrogant and smiley.

Until Florence showed up. Sylas warned me that she would be there and around him a lot. He also mentioned that she'd probably say something to him or me, but she hardly paid us any attention. Her gaze was solely trained on one of his friends on the team, and surprisingly enough, when she wasn't looking, he was looking at her.

So why he's being weird is beyond me when she hardly acknowledged or cared to talk to us.

We stop just outside the elevator. He holds my hand and doesn't let me walk any farther.

"Everything okay?" I hedge, feeling a little nervous because despite tonight not being so bad, I hardly spoke to his parents. It felt like they were intentionally avoiding me. I'm not complaining, but who knows what his mom could've told him. "We've been spending a lot of time together. If this is your way of telling me you don't—"

Sylas cups my face, leans down, and seals the space between our lips. He softly and slowly kisses me, shocking me and making the rest of my words dwindle. A moment later, I'm snapping out of my stupor and meeting his tongue with mine, letting him take his time as I do the same. I lose myself in him and I feel he's doing the same because one hand stays cupped on my cheek but the other slips around my waist, drawing me in as close as he can.

He releases a shaky breath when his lips slip from mine, and he rests his forehead against mine. "No." He kisses the tip of my nose. "I don't want you to go, Anna. I want you to stay here as my girlfriend. I mean that as my *real,* not pretend girlfriend."

I take a few steps back, letting his hands drop to his sides. "What?" I blink repeatedly, in disbelief.

"Don't *what?* me." He grins as if he were finding my reaction amusing. "You're smart enough to understand exactly *what.* But..." He studies the still-shocked expression on my face, sees that my smile is even wider than before. "In case you don't, let me bluntly put it like this: I like you, Anna. I like you a lot. I can't stop thinking about you. I can't stop dreaming about you. I can't stop wanting you. No, this isn't pretend, fake, or whatever you may think it is. This is real and so fucking honest. I want to make this real. Please tell me you do too."

My mouth parts and closes, unsure of what to say other than to smile and laugh. Sylas's lips crack into one, but he stares at me, confused.

"Is this your way of turning me down?" he jokes, but I can hear the disappointment beneath the humor.

"No." I shake my head and take a step toward him. "I was going to—I was thinking—I like you too."

There is no point in acting like he's not what I want, that I don't like him, because I do, I like him a lot. There isn't a moment I'm not thinking about him or wishing I was with him.

"Really?" He cocks a brow, taking two steps forward.

I inch closer and then he does until we're so close, his chest touches mine. He cups the side of my neck, tilting my head back. My body warms, flutters rippling all over, and my heart thunders in my ears.

"Yeah. I do."

He stares at me so endearingly, so *his*. "I know it's probably fast, but I don't want to wait for *the* moment that should define when the time is right for us to be together. This moment, you being here, feels right, too right, Anna. I want you." He drags his thumb over my jaw, repeatedly, gently. "What do you say?"

I suck in a breath, my hands going to the lapels on his tuxedo jacket. "I say this moment feels right."

"Yeah?" he asks, his voice lowering.

"Yeah." I'm smiling so big my cheeks start to ache.

He kisses me. "Remember when you told me to fuck off?"

I laugh as he pulls away and threads his thick fingers through mine, guiding me to his living room.

"Yeah, and I still don't regret it," I state proudly, feeling so giddy I'm practically bouncing as we walk, but I stop when I notice the bare enormous Christmas tree. "What's with the tree and..." My voice wavers when I notice the many bags filled with what look like decorations spilling out of them.

"I want you to have a good Christmas."

"B-but," I blubber. "You don't like this stuff and—"

"But you do. I didn't put anything up but the tree because I figured we could do it together," he sheepishly says, cheeks staining red. *Is he blushing? Is he nervous?* "I know Christmas is about to be over, but I don't mind keeping them up for a while. For as long as you want. I know this isn't anything like you spending Christmas with your family, but we can try."

My eyes prick and the bridge of my nose stings. "No, it's not, but I don't want that. I just want whatever we do. This is all I care about."

Yeah, it sucks that I haven't spoken to my parents since the last time I talked to Mom. I saw the pictures Maya posted on her socials with our parents and the entire family spending Christmas Eve together, partying and having a good time without me. It hurt but then I forgot about the ache when Sylas picked me up earlier. It didn't matter what we did or who was around. I was happy knowing I was going to be with him.

His cheeks burn brighter, and his dimples deepen. "I hope you like what I bought."

"It could've been just the tree and that would've been enough." I clear my throat, hiding the emotions thickening it. "Thank you." I spin, standing on my tiptoes, wrapping my arms around his neck as he circles his around me. I hear the sound of his rapidly beating heart, and I inhale his cologne. "This is the best Christmas ever."

"Yeah?" There's no arrogance in the tone of his voice. He just sounds proud and elated.

"Yes," I breathe, brushing my lips against his. "Wait." I jerk back. "I still haven't baked something for you."

He laughs, tugging me back to his chest. "We have all the time in the world for you to do that whenever you want. Do you want to put up the decorations now, or tomorrow?"

"Now!" I reply a little too quickly, too ecstatically. "If you're not tired. We can def—"

"No, let's do it now." He squeezes me tight, whispering against my ear, "I'm happy you told me to fuck off."

I laugh, my chest vibrating against his. "I'll do it again."

He takes my hand in his, guiding me toward the stairs. "Yeah, how about you do that while I help you out of this dress. It'd give me a reason to test the ball gag."

The pulse between my thighs picks up, and my body buzzes with anticipation.

"Merry Christmas, Anna." He smirks.

I roll my eyes, but I can't look annoyed because I'm too happy. "Merry Christmas, Sylas."

27

ANNA

I ROCK BACK AND FORTH, CAREFUL NOT TO WAKE HER
as I lean over the railing of her crib to lay her down.

Jenny pokes her head in, mouthing, *It's ready*.

Once she's flat on her back and I've made sure the swaddle is
securely wrapped around her, I quietly walk out of my room.

"Here." Jenny sets my steaming breakfast plate along with a
mug in front of me. "It's hot, just like you like it."

I force a smile, fighting against the desire to cry. I thought
being pregnant was hard, but despite how much I heard about
what comes after you give birth, I still wasn't prepared.

Clearing my throat, I raise my lips higher. "Thanks. I know
I've said this a lot but thank—"

"Shut up." She harshly glares. "I've told you to stop thanking
me. I'm here for you always. You're my best friend and that's my
niece. I'll do anything for you both. Don't forget that."

Grinding my teeth, I blow out a weary breath, dropping my
teary gaze down as I nod.

She grabs my hand and squeezes it. "It's okay. Let it all out.
I'm here for you."

And I do. I break down for the millionth time since everything ended between Sylas and me.

To be continued...
Book 2 will be released in 2026

ALSO BY E. SALVADOR

The Knights Series:

A college basketball romance series

Book 1: All I Need

Lola & TJ's story

A secret baby, he's the basketball captain, she's a live painter, slow burn romance

Book 2: Only With You

Julianna & Landon's story

An enemies to lovers with lots of banter, he tutors her, forced proximity romance

The Midnight Strike Series:

A college baseball romance series

Book 1: Please Don't Go

Josie & Danny's Story

A strangers to lovers, black cat x golden retriever, she teaches him how to swim, roommates romance

ACKNOWLEDGMENTS

This book would not have been possible to write without my husband constantly being there to cheer me on, listen to me talk about my characters, and making me many cups of coffee. Thanks for all you do and continue to do!! YOU ARE THE BEST!!

Emily, Em, I love you! I can't thank you enough for all you do! We may be miles away from each other but I've never felt closer to someone. You are a STAR!! I heart you a bunch!

Savanna, we're here again. Thank you for letting me talk your ear off about my million stories and for always being my biggest champion! You are my rock and I adore you so much!!

Anlly, thank you for being here! For all you do and for keeping me sane! Thanks for being a big cheerleader about everything and all I do, and for keeping all my book secrets!

Tammy, thank you for all your input and suggestions and translation! You were so helpful and I'm so grateful for you! Thank you a million!!

Erica, thank you for once again taking on another manuscript! You have no idea how much I appreciate you and I can't wait to share more with you!

Britt, thank you for taking on this project! You were so amazing to work with and I can't wait to work with you some more!!

Lilith, thank you for making such a beautiful cover!! I still can't get over it and won't ever stop staring at it!

And my readers, thank you so much! I wouldn't be able to continue to write without all your love and support to my characters and me! You guys are rock stars! Thank you all so much for being freaking amazing!!

Thank you for sticking around!

With Love,
E

ABOUT THE AUTHOR

E. is a Mexican-American romance author who loves a good happily ever after and iced coffee with light ice.

When E. is not overthinking or creating multiple Pinterest boards for the hundred book ideas she has, she's writing or reading. And when she's not doing any of those things, she's spending time with her two sons and husband.

Instagram/TikTok: e.salvadorauthor
Goodreads: e. salvador

www.ingramcontent.com/pod-product-compliance
Lightning Source LLC
Chambersburg PA
CBHW031040310726
48969CB00007B/2060